ACCIDENTAL MURDER

THE 14TH DETECTIVE INSPECTOR
CAROL ASHTON MYSTERY

BY CLAIRE McNAB

Bella
BOOKS

Ferndale, Michigan
2002

Bella Books, Inc.
P.O. Box 201007
Ferndale, MI 48220

Printed in the United States of America on acid-free paper
First Edition

Edited by Greg Herren
Cover designer: Bonnie Liss (Phoenix Graphics)
Cover photo by Amy Blake

ISBN 1-931513-16-3

For Sheila

Acknowledgments

With appreciation for the sterling efforts of my editor, Greg Herren, and the enviable skills of my Phantom Typesetter. And special thanks to Donna McBride.

CHAPTER ONE

The Wednesday early morning phone call came just as Carol returned from her daily run through the bushland with Olga, her neighbor's enthusiastic German Shepherd. She snatched up the receiver on the fourth ring before the answering machine could cut in. "Carol Ashton."

Detective Sergeant Mark Bourke's voice had its usual amused timbre. "Someone tumbled off the cliffs at North Head around six-thirty this morning. I've got a name — John Trelawney, but not much else. The local cops are on the scene and the Police Rescue Unit should be there by now. The victim's wife is crying foul play, so I thought you'd like to take a look, since it's so close to you."

Carol sighed as she put down the phone. It was early

autumn, and not yet too chilly to have breakfast outside on the back deck sheltered by crowding gumtrees. She'd been looking forward to sitting with her coffee and toast and the morning paper spread out on the redwood table. Sinker would be lurking nearby with his habitual high hopes of snagging one of the birds who regularly mocked his hunting efforts. The rainbow lorikeets, their feathery bodies beautiful, but decidedly garish in blue, green, violet and orange, were always particularly abusive, screeching insults the moment they spied Sinker's black and white form.

This morning she'd have to forego this small delight that helped her prepare for the morning drive to work. Traffic seemed to be becoming thicker every week. She had a fast shower, gulping black coffee as she dressed, and was making sure Sinker had adequate provisions to keep his feline self happy when the phone rang again.

"Carol Ashton."

"The inestimable Detective Inspector Carol Ashton?" inquired a warm American voice.

"That would be me." Carol found herself smiling. "And I presume this is remarkable FBI Agent Leota Woolfe."

"The very one. Carol, I'll be in Sydney tomorrow for a conference on international terrorism, and I was hoping you could keep an evening, maybe more, free for me. Sorry to spring this on you at such short notice, but I've just learned myself that I'm scheduled at the conference."

"For you, Leota, I'll cancel everything on my busy social agenda." It was almost disconcerting to hear the playfulness in her own voice.

"It's at the Wallitz Hotel in Sydney. I'll call you once I'm there and can figure out when I can steal some time. They're expecting me to be available twenty four-seven, of course, but hey, a girl's got to have a break, don't you think?"

"I do," said Carol with emphasis. "I'll wait for your call."

Hurrying to her car in the street-level carport, Carol pictured Leota Woolfe's dark skin, compact body, and the slow urgency of her kiss. Carol had met her while Carol had been in the States for a rigorous training course at Quantico, Virginia. Their relationship now was a great deal more than mutual attraction, but Carol deliberately had not thought of the future, even when Leota arranged for a transfer to overseas duty in Australia. For the past few months Leota ad been stationed in Canberra as one of the FBI representatives liaising with the Australia federal government.

Casting one last regretful glance at her tree-surrounded house, Carol turned her mind to the situation ahead. The site of the fall almost certainly meant that the victim was dead, as the cliffs plunged at least a hundred meters to the rock platform below.

The Sydney Harbour National Park was only twenty minutes away from her home in Seaforth. Carol zipped down Sydney Road, glancing with resignation at the clogged traffic on the other side heading towards the bottleneck of the Spit Bridge and the torturous drive through suburban streets towards the city. She skirted the Manly shopping area and flew up Darley Road, a steep ascent that passed the imposing presence of St. Patrick's College and then the far more utilitarian buildings of Manly Hospital.

At the crest of the hill Carol turned onto the narrow North Head Scenic Drive. On her right was bushland, on her left the anonymous military homes belonging to North Head Army Barracks. These were soon replaced by the blank surface of a high stone wall garnished with broken glass to discourage trespassers. It was early in the day for tourists. Carol saw only a few cars on the road, although she knew when the story hit the news quite a few people would be unable to resist visiting the scene of the tragedy.

Focused on finding where the police cars were parked, Carol hardly spared a glance at the wonderful views that soon appeared off the Sydney Harbour, and far away across the water the tall buildings of central Sydney glistening in the morning sunlight. The vegetation, now fully exposed to the

3

harsh winds from the ocean, had become progressively more stunted as she drove along the headland.

The scenic road ended in a one-way loop that brought all traffic back the route it had come. In the adjacent parking area Carol saw two patrol vehicles, a black four wheel drive with two people sitting in the back seat, and a couple of other cars, one parked away in a corner. A constable who looked far too young to be in uniform was waving would-be sightseers' vehicles away.

"You can't stop here," he barked at Carol, then blushed. "Oh, Inspector Ashton, I didn't realize it was you."

"It's me. Where did it happen?"

He pointed. "That way. Follow the path and look for the Rescue truck. You can't miss it."

"Apart from the patrol cars, can you account for all these vehicles?"

He frowned, then realization dawned on his face. "You mean could there be someone else here we don't know about?"

"Something like that."

"The Toyota four wheel drive belongs to the guy who fell off the cliff. That's his wife in the back, with Sid trying to calm her down. This car here is Sergeant Dent's."

"The one in the corner?"

"I dunno."

Carol suppressed her impatience. "Radio the license plate details and find out the registered owner."

"Right away," he said.

She parked her car and set off through the low shrubs. Only hardy vegetation could exist in the poor soil and exposed conditions of the headland. As if to prove this was an inhospitable environment, a brisk, cutting breeze was whipping up over the edge of the cliff, bending the brush before it. Carol pulled her jacket more tightly around her. In the shelter of the parking area the sun had been warm, but here there was a wintry bite to the air.

Joining the silent knot of people peering over the cliff,

4

Carol checked who was there: two patrol officers in uniform, a man and woman whom she assumed were local cops from the Manly Station, and a couple of members of the Police Rescue Unit. The police doctor hadn't yet arrived, nor had the crime scene personnel.

The Police Rescue truck had been backed right up to the safety fence so that a cable attached to a heavy winch could snake over the edge, joining climbing ropes that also disappeared into the void. Carol wasn't worried by heights, but even she was appalled when she glanced over the rim to see the drop down which the other two members of the Rescue team were abseiling.

The sandstone cliff, constantly assaulted by the elements, was slowly disintegrating. Huge slabs that had fallen from its face were heaped on the rock platform far below. On one sloping block the body lay, arms and legs outstretched. It seemed tiny, like a discarded toy, and the two men dangling on ropes above it like foolish risk-takers who could plunge to the bottom any moment.

The man in overalls next to Carol, who was supervising the playing out of the cable holding the cradle to which the body would be strapped, glanced over at her with a grin. "How yer goin', Carol?"

She'd known Vance Leroy for many years. "Fine," she said. "And you?"

"Can't complain. Squeaked by without the Integrity Commission gettin' me."

Carol grimaced. The Police Service was in the middle of yet another corruption scandal. Several cops with whom she'd trained had been caught up in the Commission's net.

Their conversation broke the spell that held the rest of the group silently staring over the edge. A burly man in a wrinkled brown suit held out his meaty hand. "Sergeant Richie Dent, Manly cops." He had narrow eyes that slanted downward at the outer corners, giving him a perpetually pained expression. "Don't think we've met."

"Carol Ashton."

He gave an amused grunt. "No need to tell me that, Inspector. You're famous, remember?"

Ignoring the jeering note with which he delivered this comment, Carol glanced at the woman by his side. Dent flapped a hand. "And this is Constable Karrie North, just new to the station. And we're lucky to have her, eh, Karrie?"

Constable North gave him a cold look, then nodded politely to Carol. She was tall and awkwardly made, as though her body hadn't turned out quite as intended. Or perhaps, Carol thought, it was the way she held herself, as though uncomfortably aware there was a good chance she would blunder into some object unless she took great care.

Dent said, "You'll be wanting to speak with the victim's wife, Inspector. Got her sitting back in the parking area."

"Did she see her husband fall?"

He shook his head. "She says it was too cold for her, so she waited in the car while he went off with his binoculars. He was captain, retired, she says, came up here several days a week to watch the shipping."

Carol looked around. She remembered a time when there had been no barrier to the edge, but in recent years safety fences had been erected in the locations that offered the best views. Here where they stood the wire-netting fence was waist high, and easily surmounted. There was a meter or so of rock before the sheer drop began.

"Do we know the point from which he fell?"

Dent jerked a thumb in the direction of the Police Rescue officers. "Ask them. They're the experts."

Vance Leroy was fully involved in paying out the cable from the truck, so Carol asked the question of one of the other men in overalls.

"Yeah, Inspector, we nutted it out before we drove the truck in. Didn't want to put our big feet in any evidence, did we? Still, I reckon you won't find much anyway." He pointed

6

to the other end of the fenced area. "Judging from where he landed, we calculated he probably took the dive from about there, give or take a bit."

"Did you tell this to Sergeant Dent?" asked Carol, hiding her growing irritation.

"Yeah." The man gave her a grin. "Wasn't much interested."

Carol thanked him, did a quick visual check of the area indicated, being careful not to step to close to the railing, then went back to Dent. "I want this entire area cordoned off."

Dent, looking bored, said, "Look after it, Karrie, will you?" He shoved his hands into his pockets and began a tuneless whistle.

It was not uncommon for Carol to run into this passive-aggressive stance. Some suburban cops had an automatic us-and-them response to any head office incursion onto their turf. Deciding that challenging Dent about his attitude would only encourage him, she stuck to the matter at hand. "Have you any feeling that this might be a suicide?"

"A jumper?" Dent lifted his thick shoulders. "I put the idea to his wife, but no way would she go along with it. Seems she thinks he was pushed, but she didn't come up with why or how or who." His attitude made it clear he thought her opinion was hardly worth discussing.

"Any witnesses?"

"Nope. Or at least, no one that stuck around."

"Perhaps you could have your patrol officers do a quick search."

Dent's face hardened at this, obviously seeing an implied criticism in Carol's suggestion. "Look," he said, "the guy got too close to the edge and fell over. Or maybe he *did* jump. Who knows?" Unsaid was, *Who cares?*

"There's an unidentified car in the parking area, so there well might be a witness on the headland who noticed something."

7

He gave an impatient grunt, called the two patrol officers over, instructed them to do a sweep of the immediate headland, then turned to Carol. "Satisfied?"

By now cynically amused by Dent's near insolence, she gave him a half-smile that seemed to disconcert him, but was spared any further confrontation because the cradle with its lifeless burden was winched into view. Vance maneuvered it to the ground near the truck and unclipped the cable. "A total goner from the second he went over," he observed.

The body was wrapped in a waterproof sheet, held tight by the straps cinching it securely into the cradle stretcher. Vance unfastened the top strap and flipped back the sheet. "Want to have a gander?"

Carol gave the body a quick look, knowing nothing she could observe here was going to be of much help. The post mortem would reveal the cause of death, which was almost certainly from the trauma of the fall. There was always the off chance that John Trelawney had been shot or stabbed before his trip into empty air.

He'd landed face down, so his features were unrecognizable. Carol thought she could detect a mustache. His skull was smashed and deformed, but it was still clear that he had had a fine head of steel gray hair. Incongruously, the remains of binoculars, flattened by the fall, were still on a strap around his neck.

"Doctor's here," said Dent.

The police doctor was followed, Carol saw with pleasure, by Liz Carey, head of the crime-scene team, and three of her technicians. Liz, short, square and brusque, said, "Morning, Carol. Any idea where he went over?"

Carol pointed to Karrie North, who was running crime scene tape around the boundaries of the area. "The Rescue guys think about there."

Liz gestured to her team, who moved off with the competent movements of those who know exactly what was expected of them. As Liz herself often said, "I run a bloody tight ship," and no one stayed on her team who failed to meet the standard of excellence she demanded.

"Nice day for it," Liz said to Carol, squinting up at the sky.

Above, a gray sea-eagle was riding the wind, its wings stiffly upswept as it soared on the updraft from the water. Carol had the fanciful thought that the eagle was watching them, amused at the sight of humans struggling to conquer the height with ropes and tackle. Abruptly it folded its wings and plunged, disappearing in a near-vertical dive after some prey only it could see.

Carol wished she had a leisurely day to spend enjoying such sights. She was very familiar with North Head and had spent many hours there. It was a favorite place to take visitors to Sydney to show off the splendid panorama of water, rocks and city. Along with the matching South Head, this northern headland formed a spectacular gateway into Port Jackson, with precipitous sandstone cliffs plummeting to the dark blue-black of deep ocean water. Carol had stood on this headland after fierce storms, watching the huge waves rolling in from the Pacific to obliterate themselves against the coastline with such force that her face was wet with salt spray lifted over a hundred meters by the wind.

The two Rescue Unit men who'd gone down to secure the body had climbed back up and were busy, retrieving ropes and divesting themselves of equipment. Liz and Carol went over to question them about their observations of the body and the area where it had landed. "Here, love," said one, handing Liz a set of Polaroid photographs. "Didn't think you'd want to go down there yourself, and the tide's coming in anyway, so me and Doug took some pictures for you."

Delighted, Liz flipped through them. "Mate, your blood's worth bottling. Is it too much to hope you had a good look around the site, as well?"

"Good as we could under the circumstances. We had to get the bloke out of there before the waves washed him away. I

9

didn't see anything unusual." He looked over at his companion. "Greg, did you?"

"Not a thing."

Liz made a face at Carol. "Hopeless as a crime scene, and I don't think we're going to get much up here. Any idea if it was an accident, or something more interesting?"

"I'm praying for accident," said Carol in heartfelt tones. "I don't want anything more interesting at the moment."

CHAPTER TWO

Carol made her way back to the parking area, enjoying the few moments of solitude with the company only of the wind and the raucous cry of a seagull overhead. As she approached the black Toyota, a uniformed officer opened one of the back doors and leapt out with palpable relief. "A bit hysterical, she is." He looked more closely at Carol and added hastily, "Inspector Ashton."

Anonymity was not a state that Carol could look forward to with any confidence. Over the years she'd had many high profile cases that had excited media attention. This meant she was easily recognized not only by other cops, but also by members of the general public.

Moving away from the vehicle, Carol asked if the woman

had said anything of interest while he'd been sitting with her. He shook his head. "Just very upset, you know, crying and saying how she always told him to be careful. Stuff like that."

Evelyn Trelawney turned to Carol with relief when she slid into the seat vacated by the officer. "Oh, I'm so glad you're a woman, if you know what I mean. Not that he wasn't trying to be helpful, but . . ." She made an vague gesture with one flaccid hand. "Men . . . They don't really understand, do they?"

Evelyn Trelawney had a high, piping voice, stick-thin arms and legs, and a pigeon chest that Carol always associated with chronic asthma sufferers. She was wearing a tweed skirt and a lilac blouse with a cardigan in a deeper shade of the same color. She had limp gray hair, pale blue eyes and an expression that combined anxiety and a desire to please. Her eyes and nose were red from crying, and she clutched a handful of damp paper tissues.

Carol introduced herself, and the woman nodded. "Do you want some coffee, dear?" she asked, indicating a large silver thermos flask. "The Captain always liked his coffee after he'd finished with his sightings. We came up here, two, three, sometimes four times a week. He was a captain for many years, many years. It was his hobby, you know, watching the shipping movements. Kept him interested."

Ordinarily Carol would have killed for coffee, but somehow the idea of drinking a dead man's beverage seemed macabre. "No, thank you." Then, thinking there might be a possibility some drug had been added to the thermos that could explain the fall, Carol added, "Did your husband drink coffee before he left the car?"

"Oh, no dear! The Captain was a man of very decided habits. He only had coffee *after* he returned from his sightings. Never before."

"You didn't accompany him on his sightings?"

"Well, yes, I did sometimes. I kept very quiet, of course. The Captain doesn't like to be disturbed when he's concentrating. But this morning it was so cold, and I wheeze a bit when I get chilled, so I stayed here while he —"

She broke off as tears filled her eyes.

"So you didn't see anything?"

"No, dear. But when he took so long, I went to look for him." A sob shook her body. "His favorite spot — I went there. And I couldn't see him, and then I looked over the edge, not really thinking that . . ."

"I'm so sorry for your loss, but I hope you understand I have to ask these questions."

Evelyn Trelawney blew her nose daintily, then patted Carol's hand. "I understand. You're only doing your job."

"Did your husband ever climb over the fence to get a better view?"

"Yes, dear. All the time. He had no patience for things like safety fences. Said everyone should take responsibility for their own safety. He was very adamant about that."

"And this morning, did he seem quite normal?"

"Normal?" Evelyn seemed defensive. "Why wouldn't he be normal?"

"What I mean is, was your husband preoccupied, perhaps, or not feeling as well as usual?"

This gained Carol a sharp look. "What are you saying? That he got dizzy, or something like that?"

"It is a possibility."

"The Captain was perfectly well. He hardly had a day's sickness in his entire life."

She filed away the fact that the topic of Trelawney's health seemed to cause some indignation in his wife, and changed the subject. "Did you see anyone else around, or notice a strange car? Anything unusual?"

Evelyn Trelawney gave an emphatic shake of her head. "Absolutely nothing. But I've been sitting here thinking, and I know what happened." Her soft face had a look of grim determination. "I couldn't tell that young man who was sitting with me — he wasn't a detective. I decided I needed to speak with someone who would understand." She leaned toward Carol. "Like you, Inspector."

"Please tell me."

"It could have been Dianne, you see. She's always hated the Captain. Dianne could have sneaked up here to wait for him, and then pushed him over the cliff."

She sent Carol a hopeful look. "You'll question her, won't you? I wouldn't want her to get away."

"And Dianne is . . .?"

"The Captain's daughter." She put up her thin hands. "No relation to me, thank heavens! Child of his first marriage."

"Did you actually see Dianne here, this morning?"

Evelyn shook her head emphatically. "Oh, no. She's far too cunning for that." She clasped Carol's hand with surprising strength. "You do believe me, don't you?"

Carol had lost count of the times she'd been asked that question, frequently by people who were attempting to lie convincingly. In this instance she had no idea whether this accusation was a true belief, wishful thinking, or a spiteful attempt to vilify someone Evelyn disliked.

Choosing to be diplomatic, Carol said soothingly, "We'll investigate everything fully."

There was nothing more for Carol to do at the site. When Evelyn confided that the Captain had never let her behind the wheel of the four wheel drive, Carol arranged for one of the patrol officers to take the Toyota to Manly Police Station while she herself drove Evelyn there. The media had arrived in force, as had members of the public determined to see what was happening.

Once free of the crush of vehicles, Carol asked for more information about Trelawney's daughter. Evelyn was pleased to comply. Dianne Beaton was John Trelawney's only child, and had been ten when her mother and father separated. The divorce was acrimonious. Hostilities had continued until Dianne's mother had died.

"Ruth and the Captain were never really suited," Evelyn

declared. "And then, of course, he fell in love with me, you see."

Her tears had stopped, and apart from an occasional tremble of her lips or the odd sniff, she seemed considerably calmer. "His first wife, she was a loud woman. John couldn't abide loud women. Ruth accused me of stealing him away from her, but that, of course, wasn't true. Don't smile, but when he met me he told me that it was a case of him finding his true soul mate. Ruth never understood that. Until the day she died she blamed me."

Resisting the temptation to ask why the Captain had married a loud woman when he couldn't stand such a creature, Carol asked for the daughter's address.

"Double Bay, dear. Dianne couldn't afford to live in that area — she's feckless, you know — but for the fact that her ex-husband gave her the house in the divorce settlement."

"Did Captain Trelawney see his daughter regularly?"

"Oh, yes. The Captain was punctilious about such things. He knew his duty as a father, even if Dianne had no idea of the proper respect she owed him."

"And they were on good terms recently?"

Evelyn folded her hands and bent her head to study them closely. "I believe you'll have to ask Dianne about that. All I know is that her father was furious with her, and —" She broke off to look over at Carol. "I don't accuse her lightly, you know. John was threatening to cut her out of his will. I don't know any details. He didn't discuss such things with me."

"Did he change his will?"

"No, I'm sure not." Her face full of consternation, she said, "Oh, dear. I suppose it's only proper for me to call her and say what's happened, even if she secretly knows already . . ."

Glancing over to see that Evelyn's eyes were again brimming with tears, Carol said, "I'll look after it."

"*Would* you? I'd be so grateful. She's always resented me, I'm afraid."

At the station Evelyn Trelawney's statement was typed

and signed. Constable North, who was to drive the widow in the Toyota to the Trelawneys' Balgowlah home, arranged for a patrol car to follow her for the lift back.

On her way out Evelyn caught sight of Carol and came over to say to her, "He was a handsome man, the Captain. People looked up to him. He was that kind of person, he demanded respect automatically, if you see what I mean. You'll return the photos, won't you?"

"Of course. It's just a formality to ask for them."

She nodded, satisfied, and allowed herself to be led away.

Double Bay was only a few kilometers from the Police Centre, so Carol called Bourke, told him the events of the morning and arranged for him to call on Dianne Beaton. Evelyn had assured Carol, "Dianne doesn't work, or do anything useful, just rattles around inside that mansion of hers. And Dianne's had plenty of time to get back there this morning, after she . . ." Evelyn's voice had faded away at that point as her face crumpled into a fresh flood of tears.

"Mark, when you tell Ms. Beaton about her father's death, see what you think of her reactions. Evelyn Trelawney is more than keen to accuse her of making an early morning trip to this side of the harbor with the aim of killing her father. It's seems far-fetched on the face of it, but you never know."

"You certainly don't," said Bourke with a laugh. "There's something about close familial relationships that brings out the murder in people."

Sergeant Dent intercepted Carol as she was about to leave for the city. Seeming displeased, he said, "That car in the parking area belongs to one Reginald Munson. After a bit of a search we found him halfway down the headland in the middle of the bush." His mouth twisted in a sneer. "He claims he's a birdwatcher, but I'd reckon he's a perve."

"What would interest a pervert at that location so early on a cold morning?" Carol asked.

16

Dent shrugged impatiently. "Ask him yourself. He's on his way here right now."

"Has he got a record?"

Another irritated shrug. "Doesn't seem to. Maybe he hasn't been caught, yet."

Reginald Munson was a meek, round-shouldered man in a worn duffel coat and ancient jeans. He held a binocular case in one hand and a faded baseball cap in the other. He entered the interview room cautiously. His gaze flickered in turn to the sparse furniture — a table and several battered chairs — to the faintly grubby walls, the scuffed floor, and then to Dent and lastly, Carol. She introduced herself and invited him to sit down. When he shed his coat he revealed a homemade sweater of many colors, apparently knitted from odd balls of wool.

"See here," he said, trying for truculence and succeeding only in looking apprehensive, "I was just minding my own business. You've got no call to bring me to the station."

"A man fell from the cliffs this morning."

"Yeah? Well, don't look at me. I don't know anything about it."

Dent had remained standing. Hands rammed in his pockets, he loomed over Munson. "Just exactly what were you doing on North Head, hidden in the bush?"

"I told the other cop — I was birdwatching. I go up there often."

"What sort of birds would they be? Young, attractive ones?"

Munson managed a weak smile. "The feathered sort. You wouldn't catch girls up there that time of morning." He leaned forward so he could yank a notebook out of his hip pocket. "Have a look at this. I keep a record of the birds I see."

Dent's derisive grunt indicated his opinion of Munson's notebook. "You been in trouble before?"

"No!" Munson swallowed. "I did get a ticket once for speeding . . . That's all."

Interposing before Dent could continue, Carol said, "If you go up on the headland frequently, Mr. Munson, I imagine you see other people who are regular visitors too."

"I might," he said cautiously, "but I mind my own business. I'm not one for talking much."

"Just hiding in the bush and watching, eh?" sneered Dent.

Ignoring this, Carol said to Munson, "Did you see any other vehicles?"

"When I was driving along I noticed a car parked on one of the pull-offs along the road. You know, where you can stop and look at the view."

Carol asked him for more details. Munson was unable to add more than to say it was an ordinary sedan, blue he thought, and there was no one sitting in it.

Recalling Evelyn Trelawney had stated she hadn't seen any other vehicles, Carol said, "When you parked your car was there anyone else there?"

"A black Toyota. Big thing — one of those off-the-road numbers. I didn't want to get anywhere near it, so I parked at the other end."

Dent, who'd been rocking on his feet and whistling to himself, broke in with, "Hiding, were you?"

"I wasn't hiding, but neither of them would have noticed, anyway. They were having a ding-dong fight, or at least the old guy was shouting at this woman. It was his wife, I suppose, but whoever, he was off his head, and she was crying."

"It's not likely you could hear all this while they were in the vehicle, is it?" said Dent.

"They'd both got out. While I was watching, the man grabbed her arm and was pulling her, but she didn't want to go. Red in the face, he was. He raised his hand and I thought he was going to hit her." Munson's face was apologetic. "Suppose you think I should have done something, and I would've if it

18

had gone on, but then the old guy yelled something like, 'Fuck you,' and walked off."

Dent's expression showed he was inclined not to believe this story. "And what happened then?"

"The lady got back in the car. It wasn't my business, so I took the long way around and avoided both of them."

"Had you seen them on other occasions?" Carol asked.

"Yeah, I think so. But I told you, I don't go up there to chat with people, so I don't pay any attention to them. In fact, I keep away. They scare the birds."

Further questioning didn't shake Munson's story. He'd seen no one else, apart from the occupants of the Toyota, he hadn't heard a scream or shout, nor had he noticed anything unusual or out of the way.

"Then you lot turned up," he said to Dent, adding with a hint of resentment, "I'd just spotted what I thought was a Southern Emu-Wren, but you cops frightened it away."

As he was speaking, Karrie North slid quietly into the room. She went to Dent and handed him two photographs. He gave them a quick glance, waved a dismissal to the constable, then handed the photos on to Carol.

The larger one was obviously a formal portrait taken by a professional, the smaller a snap taken outside, with the Captain standing to attention in what looked like the back yard of a house. In both, the man was glaring directly at the lens with a set face. His steel gray hair was as disciplined as his posture, and his mustache bristled vehemently under a bony, high-beaked nose. His widow had been accurate when she had said he was handsome, Carol thought, In his youth John Trelawney had probably been quite stunning.

She put the photographs down in front of Munson. "Do you recognize this man?"

"Yeah, of course I do. It was the guy fighting with his wife in the parking area." With what seemed to be an attempt at a jocular remark, Munson added, "Bit of a bastard, eh?"

"A dead bastard," said Dent quellingly. "Sure you didn't push him off the cliff?"

"I never went near him. Why would I?" He looked to Carol for help. "I didn't even know the bloke."

"Hmmm," said Dent, rocking heel to toe, hands back in his pockets.

"Look, I want out of here. You can't make me stay."

Dent frowned at him for a long moment, then said, "We need a formal written statement from you, signed, before you can leave." He leaned his bulky body closer to the seated man. "You have a problem with that?"

Munson put his hands up as if he thought Dent was about to going to strike him. "Okay, okay."

Carol kept her face blank. She disliked bullies, and Richie Dent was plainly getting considerable pleasure out of intimidating this witness. "I'd like a copy of Mr. Munson's statement faxed to me as soon as it's available," she said.

"You're leaving us, Inspector?" Dent almost smiled.

Amused that he was so obviously delighted to be rid of her, Carol said, "Unless there's something . . .?"

"We've got everything under control."

Leaving Munson to make his formal statement, Carol located Constable North to ask her to make sure the photographs were returned to Evelyn Trelawney after copies had been made, then she went to her car.

The traffic had subsided to moderate levels, so Carol could take pleasure in contemplating the blue expanse of Middle Harbour as she swooped down to Spit Bridge, and, closer to the city, the gray arch of the Sydney Harbour Bridge and the incomparable views of the harbor and Opera House.

Serenity wasn't something Carol expected to feel, but this morning she felt content, calm. Her work schedule was extremely heavy, but several cases were in the winding-up stage and the rest appeared well under control. And Leota was coming to town. She smiled to herself.

Life was good.

CHAPTER THREE

Once in her utilitarian office with its standard-issue furniture and drab walls, Carol didn't feel quite so serene. She frowned at her desk, surveying the routine paperwork that threatened to overwhelm it. Deciding to tame the flood, she sat down with resolution, and plunged in. Working steadily, and refusing to be deflected by the phone calls that punctuated her efforts, she reduced the stack in her in-tray to a shadow of its former self.

Of course, she could never match Mark Bourke's desk, which was quite unnaturally tidy. Indeed, she'd often seen his in-tray entirely empty. With anyone else, Carol would have suspected that the inward flow of paper memos, notices and admonishments had been diverted to a bottom drawer, but in

Mark's case she knew with certainty that he'd dealt with each and every one.

She was ready for a break when Liz Carey called to say that her team had essentially found nothing of note at the North Head site. "We've got a lot of fingerprints, Carol, the majority partials, from the metal railing at the lookout. We're checking them out, but most will be anonymous members of the public there for the scenery, not to push someone over the drop. We scoured the whole area, but it's solid rock, so no footprints, scuff marks, or the like. No drops of blood, no discarded weapons — nada, nix, nothing."

"Pretty well a waste of time, then?"

"Oh, I wouldn't say that," said Liz. "The view was nice."

As Carol rang off, Bourke appeared at her door. "Hope you aren't pinning your hopes on Dianne Beaton as a suspect," he said. "I was hardly inside her front door before she announced that she already knew about her father's death and she had an alibi."

"Did Evelyn Trelawney call her?"

"No, she heard a news bulletin that someone had been killed at North Head, and knowing her father was up there most days, she called Manly cops and was told the news by one Richie Dent."

Hearing something in Bourke's voice when he said the name, Carol said, "Do you know Dent?"

"Afraid I do. He's just about makes it as a cop, but he's a nasty bit of work. A bully, holds grudges, and always gets even if he can."

Carol leaned back, putting the cap on her gold fountain pen. "Let's go out and get coffee, Mark. I really don't think I can face the black tar we have here."

They strolled through warm autumn sunshine in companionable silence to Oxford Street, settling on spindly chairs at a minuscule table in a pokey little coffee shop that sold Bourke's favorite cream buns. While Bourke demolished two buns in quick order, Carol toyed with a delicate pastry and watched the wonderful variety of people passing by the window of the coffee shop. Darlinghurst was a cosmopolitan suburb, filled with a zest for living that attracted both gay and straight to the area.

Carol took a sip of her black coffee, appreciating it all the more because she'd gulped down the police approximation of coffee earlier. She looked over at Bourke, who was stirring sugar into his cappuccino. "You've got cream on the end of your nose," she said.

"Jeez, do I?"

Carol had to laugh at his enthusiastic scrubbing with his handkerchief. Bourke was always, like his desk, neat and organized, so any crack in this perfection was amusing to her. She wondered how he coped with Karli, his young daughter, who was at an age when making a mess with food or toys was second nature.

"Have you trained Karli to pick up after herself yet?" she said with a grin.

Bourke smiled indulgently. "She's too little. Have I shown you the latest photos Pat took? There's a beauty of her in her wading pool."

"You have, at least twice."

Bourke cocked his head. "Were you like this about David, when he was a toddler? Besotted, like me?" His expression changed. "I'm sorry, Carol, I shouldn't have —"

"It's okay."

Unspoken between them was the fact Carol had left her husband, Justin Hart, and her son. David, now a teenager, had been brought up by her ex-husband and his second wife. Not fighting for custody of David was a decision Carol bitterly regretted. She had come to terms with the grievous reality that her action had made her, at best, into a part-time parent who'd had only a minimal influence upon her son's life.

Clearly embarrassed, Bourke said, "Let's get down to business before I say anything else unacceptable."

"Did Dianne Beaton seem upset?"

"Hard to tell. She's one of those people with a glassy surface, if you know what I mean. Early forties, hard face, hard eyes. *Said* she was devastated by her father's death, but didn't look it."

"I know her husband's dead, but does she have any children?"

"No kids."

"Did she mention Evelyn Trelawney?"

Amused, Bourke said, "Only in the most derogatory way."

"And her father?"

"Now she did say something interesting about him. It appears, at least in her opinion, that he was showing signs of Alzheimer's. She said he was forgetful, sometimes irrational, and had bouts of rage where he threw things around. I gather his wife didn't mention this?"

"No suggestion of it at all. If this is true, Trelawney could have become confused about where he was, and stepped off into thin air." She signaled for another coffee.

"Me too," called Bourke. "And another bun, please."

"Mark," said Carol severely, "Pat told me you were on a diet."

He patted his stomach. "Still flat, Carol." When she raised an eyebrow he added, "Well . . . flat-ish. I'm only carrying an extra kilo or so."

"It's the *or so* that's important."

He sighed. "It's people like you that drive me mad. You can eat anything and stay thin. Me? I've had to join a gym to try and lose some weight." He ran a hand over his short-cropped hair. "And you don't have to worry about going bald. Totally unfair, if you ask me."

The two coffees and Bourke's cream bun arrived. While he ate it, Carol said, "Trelawney's death could have been left to the local cops. It's almost certainly an accident. He and his wife had words before he stalked off to see his precious shipping movements. It's obvious he was in a foul mood, which could have made him careless, or, if Dianne Beaton is right about Alzheimer's, perhaps he became befuddled and didn't realize he was on the edge of a cliff."

She filled him with the details of Reginald Munson's statement, adding that Evelyn Trelawney had neglected to mention the argument with her husband.

Bourke said, "She might have been ashamed to mention that his mind was going. People do put up a pretence that everything's normal."

"We need the post mortem results. Apart from the possibility of Alzheimer's disease, he may have had drugs or alcohol in his system that might have made an accident more likely."

Bourke grinned. "An accident would be helpful. We've got enough on our plate at the moment without another homicide."

He was right, Carol thought. There had been a sudden, inexplicable spike in the number of suspicious deaths reported over the last month. Resources were stretched trying to cover the investigations.

"Just in case Trelawney isn't a simple case of carelessness," said Carol, "what's his daughter's alibi?"

"Apparently the couple next door to her insist on blasting out loud music very early in the day, and when they started at six-thirty this morning she decided she'd had enough, so she called the cops. About the time her dad was taking his high dive Dianne Beaton, her inconsiderate neighbors and a couple of patrol officers were involved in a very vocal confrontation."

"You've checked this out?"

"I have. The Schmitts, who apparently thrive on Wagner at very high decibels, were quite vehement that they had the constitutional right to play music whenever and however they desired. This didn't go down well with Ms. Beaton, and the three of them almost came to blows. Quite a scene — and a perfect alibi."

Carol checked her watch and groaned. "Hell, I've got a meeting with Edgar in twenty minutes."

"Good luck," said Bourke with sympathy. Superintendent Edgar had never been one of Carol's fans. She had every reason to believe it was he who'd made sure her chances of promotion to chief inspector had been put on hold.

Carol and Bourke walked briskly back to the Police Centre, with Carol mentally reviewing the cases her team was handling. The volume was noteworthy, and Edgar would be insisting even more emphatically on an excellent clear-up rate that would reflect well on him. Besides that perennial demand, she couldn't see any particular case that might warrant the super's personal interest. Superintendent Edgar always took steps to assure that blame for problems or mistakes was laid on others, not on him.

Carol had made few missteps, and none career-ending, with one notable exception; an international serial killer had slipped through Carol's fingers. Apart from that embarrassment, Carol could boast of an enviable record of arrests and convictions, and had a high media profile that gave her much attention, usually favorable.

As they neared the Centre, Bourke said, "You'll never guess who I ran into last night at the gym."

"If I'll never guess, I won't try."

"You take all the fun out of it, Carol. It was Ren Downing."

"Ren? I haven't seen him for ages."

"Well, I believe you'll be seeing him soon. He says he's got something to discuss with you."

Renfrew Downing had been a cop, and a good one. A contemporary of Carol's, they'd been stationed together in their early careers. Downing was openly gay. Although protected by law from discrimination, he eventually found the macho, testosterone-drenched camaraderie of many male cops too wearng to put up with, so he'd resigned from the Police Service to set up as a private investigator.

Ren Downing had taken a partner, another ex-cop, Gemma Pate, and together they had developed Downing & Pate into a widely known and admired investigative service, specializing in fraud, business espionage, and security measures at the corporate level.

Carol became aware that Bourke's blunt-featured face was set in a scowl. This was so out of character that she said, "What in the hell's the matter with you?"

"I've got a feeling Ren is going to offer you a job."

"What? As a P.I? You've got to be kidding."

Scoffing at the idea didn't lighten Bourke's expression. "Kidding about what, Carol? That he'd offer you a job, or that you'd accept it?"

Carol laughed. "He won't."

"You know you'd been fed up before, and thought of getting out. You've said as much, and this wouldn't be a bad move."

She snorted derisively, but secretly had to agree. There'd been times when she'd chafed under the restrictions and pressures of her position, office politics, and the need to deal with the not-so-subtle demands of those in the public who considered themselves VIPs. If she were to leave the Police Service, Downing and Pate might present an excellent opportunity. The company was run with integrity and efficiency, growing in both size and reputation over the past few years.

"No way, Mark," said Carol. "Without the authority of the police behind me, how would I get people to jump when I said jump? And besides, I seriously doubt that Ren is going to offer me anything. If he does, you'll be the very first to know."

Leaving Bourke, who still looked glum, Carol went back to her office to pick up the necessary files for her meeting. Anne Newsome was there writing a note to her.

"Your Aunt Sarah just rang," Anne said.

"Is it something urgent? I've got a meeting with the super."

"She didn't say it was urgent, but there was something in her voice . . ."

Carol respected Anne's instincts. "Okay, thanks, I'll call her back right now."

As Carol dialed the Blue Mountains number she visualized Aunt Sarah's old-fashioned kitchen, warm and always filled with delicious smells. It almost made her hungry just to think of the huge wooden table that dominated the room where she had sat countless times, both as child and adult. Her fondest memories were of many cold winter afternoons, when Aunt Sarah would bustle around serving hot scones dripping with melted butter.

"Aunt? It's Carol."

"Oh, Carol, thank you for calling back."

Frowning at the strain in her aunt's voice, Carol said, "What's the matter?"

"I was just wondering if I could spend a few days with you."

"Of course, any time. You've got a key, so just turn up when you're ready."

"Thank you, darling. I'll get the train down, and a taxi to your place."

"Something's wrong. Tell me what it is."

There was silence at the other end of the line, then her aunt said, "It's probably nothing, but there's a lump in my breast, and my doctor up here suggested I go to a breast clinic in Sydney."

Keeping her voice light, Carol said, "Wise move. When can I expect you?"

"It's silly, I know, but Dr. Harab said there was some urgency. I've got an appointment at the clinic tomorrow."

"I'll see you tonight, then. We'll go out." Carol chuckled. "I won't subject you to my cooking."

When she rang off she didn't move to pick up the files she needed for the meeting, but stood looking out the window. For the first time in her life she'd heard fear in Aunt Sarah's voice, and it chilled her.

CHAPTER FOUR

Superintendent Edgar was smoothly affable, but Carol was not deceived. Beneath that thick silver hair and cordial, faintly smug expression was a ruthless, driven individual who would step on anyone who got in the way of his ambitions. For the most part Carol's career had reflected well on him. She had no illusions he would be there to support her, should she have a spectacular failure

"Busy few weeks, Carol?" he said, waving her to a chair.

"You can say that again." She handed him a current list of active cases. "And there's another to add, a John Trelawney fell to his death off North Head early this morning."

"Not an accident?"

"It seems to be. His wife, who was waiting in the car for

him while he went off to watch shipping movements — he was a retired captain — is saying he was pushed, but so far there's no evidence of that. No witnesses to the fall, but Manly station's involved, and they're still looking. Basically we're all waiting for the post mortem results."

Edgar pinched his upper lip thoughtfully. "Sounds just like the one Saul Block had in the Blue Mountains last year. D'you know Saul?"

"I do," said Carol. Block was a clone of Superintendent Edgar in many ways, although not quite so successful in climbing the promotion ladder.

"Saul's a good mate of mine," said Edgar expansively. "He had serious doubts about this so-called accident. Seems this guy who was out jogging at sunrise pitched off Govetts Leap at Blackheath while his wife sat in a car nearby, waiting for him. Saul said he couldn't see any reason for the guy to stop at the lookout at all."

Carol knew the mountain area well, and had been to Govetts Leap, a high lookout that gave a spectacular view of part of the Blue Mountains National Park. "Maybe he was just appreciating the view."

"There wasn't one. It was very foggy that morning, so why bother looking at nothing?" The Superintendent gave a grunt. "Sounds suss, doesn't it? Still, the inquest found his death an accident, and the insurance company paid up. The whole thing didn't sit well with Saul. He said he was sure the wife was involved some way, but couldn't prove it. How about this one of yours, Carol? Could the wife have done it?"

"Evelyn Trelawney's what you'd call a little old lady," said Carol. "Even so, I suppose anything's possible."

"With you ladies, anything is," declared Edgar heartily. "Thanks to this women's lib thing, the delicate sex is slicing and dicing with the best of them. Have you seen the crime statistics on teenage girls? It's frightening."

Carol steered the conversation back to his review of the current cases.

31

"Better clear-up rate!" Edgar stabbed the list with a well-manicured, square forefinger. "We don't want the blasted media jumping on us over this issue. I want the figures looking good. Understand what I mean?"

She did, perfectly. Superintendent Edgar would deny it if asked, but he was not at all averse to the use of creative means to massage the figures to give more favorable results.

They discussed the outstanding cases for ten minutes more, then Carol was dismissed with a glib smile and an injunction to, "Keep up the good work."

On the way back to her office she ran into Bourke. "Super on the warpath?" he asked.

"Not as yet. He wants every case solved and in the case-closed column quick smart, but he always wants that."

Following Carol into her office, Bourke said, "The post mortem on John Trelawney won't be until Monday. Jeff Duke's on vacation, everyone's working double shifts, and the bodies are practically stacking up in the hallway."

"Great," said Carol with a grimace. "I was hoping to finalize the material for the inquest as soon as possible, so I could pretty well close the file."

"You know," said Bourke, "it's just occurred to me that this is very like the Bruehl death at the Gap."

Frowning, Carol said, "Bruehl? It doesn't ring a bell."

"That's because you were gallivanting around the States at the time," said Bourke. "Here's the scenario: Paulette Bruehl of Wollongong is visiting Sydney with her husband, and early this morning she's sightseeing at the Gap. Somehow she manages to somersault over the cliff and kill herself, all this while her husband's half a block away, chatting to someone."

"Suicide?"

The Gap, an indentation on the seaward side of South Head, had had many suicides over the years. The drop was a brutal one, ending with tumbled rocks that were ceaselessly pounded by the ocean swell. Carol had a theory that the rhythm and power of the constantly breaking waves created an almost hypnotic effect that tended to pull even those not entirely resolved on self-destruction to their deaths.

"Suicide didn't seem likely," said Bourke. "According to everyone who knew her, Paulette Breuhl was a sunny, cheerful sort. Unfortunately, there were no witnesses. And no evidence the husband had anything to do with it, especially as he managed to strike up a conversation with a passerby at about the critical time. There was an insurance policy, but it wasn't a particularly large one. The inquest found death by misadventure, even though she had to make the effort to climb over the safety rail in order to fall."

"Maybe she slipped while taking photographs."

Shaking his head, Bourke said, "No camera."

"So what's the connection with Trelawney?"

Bourke shrugged. "On the face of it, there isn't one." With a smile he added, "I've got an odd feeling about this case. Chalk it up to male intuition."

"The Superintendent just told me that there was another similar fall last year at Govetts Leap in the Blue Mountains."

"See," said Bourke in triumph. "I told you there was a pattern."

"What are you saying, Mark? That it's synchronicity? That quite independently, three spouses decide to toss their nearest and dearest over the nearest cliff?"

"Let's see if there's a fourth one," said Bourke. "Then you'll have to admit that something's going on."

Carol raised an eyebrow. "If you're right, what makes you think the fourth one hasn't already occurred? And the fifth and sixth? They don't all have to be in Sydney, you know."

"Cheaper and easier than divorce," said Bourke, laughing, "but hell on the crime figures."

* * * * *

The afternoon passed in a blur of meetings, reports and, when Terry Roham knocked on her door very late in the day, an unasked for opportunity for career counseling. Roham was the newest member of her team, and was clearly anxious to earn her favor, but usually made this so obvious that Carol found herself faintly irritated, instead of wholeheartedly impressed by his zeal. Aware of this, she always tried to be more than fair to him.

"Yes, Terry, what can I do for you?"

He came in, shutting the office door behind him. He was tall, with tightly-curled hair cut extremely short, and a soft, unformed face that still needed time and experience to give it maturity. Carol often had the impression that Terry Roham's energy and enthusiasm were barely under control, and would burst out any moment in some spontaneous, and possibly instantly regretted, action. Up to now his impetuosity hadn't led to serious mistakes at work, but Carol and Bourke had agreed that it was wise to keep this particular young man under close supervision.

"I've got a complaint," he blurted out.

"About what?"

"Well, maybe not a complaint, more a concern."

Carol gestured for him to sit, but when he did he jiggled around so much she felt like leaning over and putting a firm hand on his head to steady him.

"Terry, I can't help you unless you tell me what the matter is."

"It's Sergeant Bourke."

"You have a problem with Mark Bourke?" Carol could hardly imagine what this might be. Certainly Bourke had high standards, and wouldn't accept anything but a totally professional attitude in the team, but he was notably circumspect in his criticisms and very supportive of anyone willing to work hard.

"Look, this is confidential, right?"

"If you have a formal complaint, there are set procedures

to be followed, so in that sense I can't guarantee complete confidentiality."

Carol's matter-of-fact tone seemed to disconcert Roham. "Hey, I'm not talking about making this official."

"It would help," said Carol dryly, "if I knew what you were talking about."

"Oh, hell!" He wriggled his shoulders. "It's going to sound stupid, like I'm a kid whinging about something, but it's that the Sarge is always favoring Anne, and not giving me a fair go."

He sat back, his lips in a tight line, as though already sorry he'd said that much.

"Anne has been here much longer, and has more experience than you have, Terry."

"And how am I going to get the experience if I don't get a chance to learn?"

"Apart from Anne, do you feel that Mark Bourke is favoring anyone else?"

Roham almost pouted, looking so ridiculously young that Carol had a glimpse of what he would have been like as a little kid. "I'd have to say yes. Miles Li for one, and maybe Dennis. But Anne's the one I notice most."

Anne, Carol could have pointed out to him, was by far the most able of all the constables in her age group. There were good reasons for Bourke to give Anne Newsome greater responsibilities. She was dependable, intelligent and had excellent interviewing techniques. More, she had that something extra that makes a good detective a great one.

"Could you give me some specific examples?"

Roham dug in his trouser pocket and produced a folded sheet of paper. Smoothing it out, he said, "I've noted instances where it seems to me Anne was given special treatment."

Putting out her hand, Carol said, "May I see?" She glanced down the list and stifled a sigh. Resentment had been building in Terry Roham for quite some time. "Let's discuss these one by one."

Roham glanced at his watch. "Do you have the time to spare? I know you're busy."

Carol hid a grin. It was getting late, and Roham's manner indicated he hadn't counted on spending too much time in Carol's office. "I've got the time."

She took him through each incident. Most were, as Carol expected, of minor nature, but she had to admit that if the items listed were accurate, there were a couple of times where Bourke appeared to have deliberately shut Roham out.

"You say you don't want to make an official complaint. What would you like me to do?"

"Talk to the Sarge. Set him straight, so I get my fair share of the action. Half the time I'm stuck on the end of a telephone while everyone else is out doing something interesting."

"Have you told Mark specifically what is making you unhappy about the allocation of duties?"

When Roham shook his head, she asked, "Why not?"

"To begin with, the things I'm worried about sound so petty, and it's only when you look at the whole pattern that you can see what's happening. And also, frankly, I didn't think he'd listen to me."

"Have you discussed this with anyone else?"

He shuffled his feet. "I might have mentioned it to friends ..." He sneaked another look at his watch. "Look, I don't want to make a big deal out of this. All I'm asking is for you to talk with him." Roham leaned forward, very intense. "Believe me, I want to do well at this job, and I know I've got a long way to go, but how can I get there if I'm not given the chance?"

"Okay, but after I speak with Mark, the three of us need to discuss the whole matter."

Roham was already on his feet, clearly late for some important date. "Thank you," he said. "Do you mind if I ..." He gestured toward the door.

Carol smiled. "Go? Not at all."

Putting Terry Roham on her action list for the next day,

she checked the time herself. Carol had organized to take Thursday morning off, and if necessary the rest of the day if Aunt Sarah needed her. She'd worked at high concentration all afternoon to finalize outstanding matters, but even when fully occupied, concern about her aunt had leaked constantly into her thoughts.

She dialed a number and drummed her fingers while it rang. When the cool, familiar voice answered, she said, "Sybil, it's Carol. Sorry to bother you when I know you've just got home, but it's about Aunt Sarah."

"Is something wrong? I was talking with her a few days ago and everything was fine."

Apart from David, Aunt Sarah was Carol's only close blood relative. Carol loved her unreservedly, but sometimes thought Sybil had a better relationship with her aunt than she did.

Too often in her work Carol had been forced to be the bearer of bad news. She had come to believe in most cases the direct approach was preferable. "It may be a false alarm, but there's a lump in Aunt Sarah's breast and her local doctor's sent her down to a clinic here in Sydney. I'm driving her to a nine-thirty appointment."

"Oh, Carol . . ."

"She should be at my place by now. Why don't you give her a ring?"

"I will. Straight away. Is there anything I can do? I could take time off from teaching if it's difficult for you tomorrow morning."

"Thanks, but I've got it under control."

"Will you let me know what happens?"

Carol thought, when did we become so formal with each other? When did we begin to talk like strangers? Aloud she said, "As soon as I know anything."

A few more comments, and the call was over. Carol was staring unseeingly at her desk, as close to brooding as she ever allowed herself to be, when the phone rang. It was Leota Woolfe, a fact that put a ironic smile on Carol's face.

"Off with the old and on with the new," Carol said.

"What?"

"Nothing important. Just being philosophical." To head off any question that Leota, ever the investigator, might pose, Carol went on, "Are we setting up a date already? I thought you had to arrive in Sydney first."

"I've arrived already. Ran guard duty on an American businessman visiting Canberra who'd received a credible death threat, and who had to get back to Sydney today. I volunteered to baby-sit him in a New York minute, just to get close to you, Carol. I'm free tonight, how about you?"

"Oh, hell," said Carol, "I'm not."

"Nothing you can reschedule? I'm worth it, I promise you."

The warm honey of Leota's voice was more than convincing. Maybe, Carol thought, after dinner with Aunt Sarah I could have a late supper with Leota . . .

Abruptly ashamed to be thinking so much of her own pleasure, when Aunt Sarah was facing a potential threat to her life, Carol said, "It's a family emergency. I'm sorry, Leota, really I am. Can we speak tomorrow? I should be able to tell you more then."

She'd be out of the office next morning, Carol told Leota, and possibly for the whole day. They chatted affectionately for a few moments, then rang off. As she gathered her things to leave for home, Carol thought how many times she'd promised both Leota and Aunt Sarah that they would meet, but somehow it had never worked out. And even if Leota *had* known her aunt, Carol felt she couldn't give out any personal information unless Aunt Sarah had said it was okay. Carol hadn't even told Mark Bourke, and he loved Aunt Sarah dearly.

Just before she left she called her own home number to find out what type of restaurant Aunt Sarah wanted her to book for dinner. To Carol's relief, her aunt sounded much more like her usual self, announcing she'd arrived mid-afternoon, had checked Carol's cupboards, and had promptly gone to the nearest supermarket to stock up on essentials.

"I've got essentials, aunt! Black coffee and cat food for Sinker."

"You're not eating right, Carol. I've said it before and I don't doubt I'll be saying it again. All you had were frozen dinners." Her tone was scandalized. "and a few cans of soup. No multi-grain breakfast cereal, precious little fresh fruit, a couple of eggs past their use-by date. It's not good enough!"

Having elicited that a local Italian restaurant would be more than satisfactory, Carol was about to hang up when her aunt said, "Darling, I've taken the liberty of asking Sybil to join us. She called me a few minutes ago, and I hoped you wouldn't mind . . ."

"Of course not," said Carol, minding.

She rang the restaurant and made a booking for three at eight o'clock, and after checking again that she'd covered anything urgent for the next day, she left for home.

As she drove on auto-pilot, Carol thought about the contrast between Sybil and Leota. Sybil knew her so well, knew her strengths and weaknesses, knew the chinks in her armor. Leota was a stranger to much of Carol's life, as Carol was to Leota's. There was, of course, the exhilaration of solving the mystery of the other person, but in times of trouble, there was also the comfort of having someone who understood you well, to whom you need make no explanations.

The blast of an impatient horn behind her made Carol realize the traffic light had turned green. As she accelerated, she remembered that Sybil's favorite color was green. She had no idea what Leota's favorite color might be.

She didn't want to see Sybil tonight, knowing her presence would make Carol feel both easy and awkward at the same time. Shared history made it altogether impossible to be indifferent, but Carol was hoping for a time when she would achieve a measure of detachment and cool regard.

"Not much progress in that area yet," she said to the glowing red lights of the vehicle in front of her, "but tonight . . . tonight I make great strides. Just watch me."

CHAPTER FIVE

"I'm not talking about my health until Sybil arrives," said Aunt Sarah as soon as Carol walked through the front door. With the hall light behind her, Aunt Sarah's springy white hair glowed like a corona. "No, better, I'm not talking about it until the three of us are at the restaurant."

Turning to lead the way down the hall, her aunt continued over her shoulder, "Actually, it's morbid, really, to talk about illness non-stop, don't you agree? I've hardly had a day's sickness in my life, and I don't intend to start now."

Reaching the kitchen she swung around to say, "And I said to Dr. Harab that I'd go along with further prodding and probing, just to settle any worries, but this is just a false alarm, and doesn't deserve a moment's thought."

"Slow down," said Carol.

Her aunt looked taken aback, then amused. "I am raving on, aren't I? I confess it's thrown me a bit, darling. But I really do believe — okay, fervently hope — that it's nothing but some stupid little cyst."

To Carol her aunt looked vibrantly alive, her face flushed with health, her green eyes clear, her rather chubby figure straight-backed and full of energetic movement.

"What exactly did your doctor say?"

"You're not sneaking in a medical question. We'll discuss it later." She regarded her niece approvingly. "At least you're dressing with a little color these days," she said, eyeing the heavy rose silk of Carol's shirt, "although you need to get out of those severe suits."

"I don't see myself going to a homicide investigation wearing ruffles and bows."

"I meant you could wear something along these lines." Her aunt spread her arms. "It's got a bit of color, and it's comfortable. Absolutely ideal for your line of work."

As she was wearing one of her trademark bright overalls in chrome yellow, Carol had to smile. "I'll leave it to you to brighten up the world," she said.

And brighten up Carol's world was what her adored Aunt Sarah did. Carol couldn't imagine what a world would be like without her aunt's hearty laugh, her enthusiastic embrace of life.

Aunt Sarah plopped herself on one of the high-backed stools at the breakfast bar. "How was your day?"

"Busy."

"Dead bodies, I suppose."

"It does come with the territory."

Sinker came sliding gracefully through the state-of-the-art cat door Carol had recently installed. He took one look at Aunt Sarah and headed her way. "A cat of discrimination," said his target approvingly.

"He knows you're a pushover," Carol pointed out. "A few plaintive cries and you'll do whatever he wants."

"And you don't?"

Smiling, Carol admitted, "Maybe I do, but at least I put up the show of being in charge."

The front door bell chimed. Aunt Sarah raised her eyebrows. "That'll be Sybil. Easier for you if I let her in?"

"Of course not. Where did you get that idea?"

"I could see your expression, darling. Not what I'd call wholehearted welcome."

Carol shook her head, and went down the hall. She could see a glimpse of Sybil's red hair through the circular etched pane set into the door. Putting her hand on the knob she was mildly irritated to find she was consciously thinking of the impression she was about to make.

As she opened the door she wondered why she felt this way. Even when they had first separated and Sybil had retreated to her house at the beach, there hadn't been the tension that Carol sensed between them now.

"Sybil, hi. Come on in." Carol stepped out of the way, knowing she was avoiding the problem of having to decide whether a friendly embrace would be appropriate at this point, or, indeed, if Sybil expected such a gesture from her.

"Sybil!" Aunt Sarah embraced her warmly. "Have you got those women of yours chattering away in English yet?"

"Some of them."

When Carol had first met Sybil she'd been a high school English teacher. Now she was involved in giving non-English-speaking migrant women the language skills to cope with their lives in a new and strange country.

Watching them laughing over an amusing story from the classroom, Carol thought how little Sybil had changed from their first meeting. She was still slim, russet-haired, and graceful. There was something different, though. She'd become stronger, tougher and more independent. It had taken a long time for Carol to realize that when they'd lived together how often Sybil had gone along with what Carol wanted, rather than assert herself. With a rueful smile she thought how those days were well over. Carol couldn't imagine Sybil acquiescing to anything she didn't accept or want.

"I'm starving," said Aunt Sarah. Looking down at the startling yellow of her overalls, she said, "Do I have to change?"

"It's a neighborhood restaurant, aunt. I think you can pretty well wear anything there."

"This is not *anything*," she said severely. "I have these specially made for me. You don't think you can just walk into a shop and buy them, do you?"

Carol grinned. Aunt Sarah pointed a warning finger at her. "Don't say what you're thinking, Carol. I know it's unnecessarily disparaging."

Carol laughed, but a cold current touched her. *You can't have cancer*, Carol thought. *It's just not possible.*

Luigi's had standard Italian restaurant décor, but the food was sublime. As always, the room was filled with a crush of people and warm conversation. Carol had requested her favorite table in a corner. Maria, Luigi's wife, scattered comments and greetings to patrons as she led Carol, Aunt Sarah and Sybil through the narrow route between the tables.

Once seated, Aunt Sarah refused to discuss her health until they had ordered. "Pasta is an excellent carbohydrate, Carol," she pointed out as she viewed the menu, "and combined with a little tomato, basil, olive oil, whatever, it makes an excellent meal. You might bear that in mind. It takes very little time to prepare."

"Aunt Sarah doesn't think I'm eating well," Carol remarked to Sybil.

44

"She isn't. No wonder there's no meat on her bones." She glared at her niece. "You're not going to tell me you have an eating disorder, are you?"

Carol laughed. "Oh, quite the opposite, I'm afraid."

While they were still poring over the menu, a bottle of rough red appeared on the table, "Compliments of the house," said Luigi, beaming at them. "For the beautiful ladies."

Carol chose a main course of pasta and lobster, approved by Aunt Sarah as being an excellent, healthy choice. "I aim to have one of those wicked Italian desserts," said Carol, so don't get too pleased with me yet."

After they had all placed their orders, Carol said, "Come on, aunt, all the details. You promised."

"Oh, very well, but I'm sure it's a lot of fuss about nothing. Waste of time, really."

"Your doctor doesn't think so," said Sybil, "and I don't believe you do either."

To Carol, her aunt seemed to shrink a little. Biting her lip, she said, "All right, here it is from go to whoa. I went in for my annual mammogram — " She broke off to inquire, "You do have regular mammograms, don't you both?"

"Of course we do," Sybil said, "but let's get back to you."

"I went in for my mammogram, and waited afterwards as usual, expecting to be told everything was normal. But this time it wasn't. The doctor came in and said he wanted repeat views of my right breast. I knew then something was wrong."

"And?" prompted Carol.

"And they did another mammogram, and I waited some more, and then they came and said the doctor wanted to see me in his office. He was very nice. He told me something was there, but it was only small, less than the size of a pea, and that I'd need a biopsy to find out what it was, for sure."

Sybil's concerned expression belied her conversational tone. "You've had the biopsy, I suppose."

"No, I haven't. Not yet. A full report went to my own Dr.

Harab who, after we discussed all the options for treatment, convinced me it would be best to come to Sydney to go to a clinic that treats hundreds of cases a year."

There was a pause, then Sybil said, "What are the options?"

Aunt Sarah took a sip of her red wine. "It depends on the type of breast cancer and the stage — whether it's spread to the lymph nodes under my arm, or not. Once they know that, then the decision is whether to have the whole breast removed, or just take out the lump and tissue around it."

This time she took a substantial gulp of wine before continuing, "If it *is* cancer — and it may not be — then I'll have the operation immediately. Depending on what they find, it'll be a lumpectomy, or . . ." Her mouth trembled.

Carol put her hand on her aunt's. "Aunt Sarah, even if it is bad news, at least you know, and can do something about it. Breast cancer's curable, don't forget that."

"I know it is, darling, but I have to admit this has shaken me a little. There's something about the word cancer that . . ." With an obvious effort, she managed a smile. "Don't look so tragic, you two. I'm not going to drop my bundle over this. What needs to be done is going to be done. Now, let's talk about more pleasant things. Sybil, did I tell you the Eco-Crones are getting a website?"

"What a great idea."

"We think so. We've got big plans in the works." She grinned at Carol. "You'll approve, Carol. We're even thinking long-term of going international. Eco-Crones on every continent — that's our aim."

"Oh, God," said Carol, "you'll be jetting all over the world, will you?" She had a vision of her aunt flung into some dire prison cell in a third-world country. "I don't think it's altogether a very good idea."

"Oh, come on," Sybil said, "where's your sense of adventure?"

Clearly delighted to get a rise out of Carol, Aunt Sarah

said, "There's no need for you to get upset this early in the piece. Eco-Crones are not fully established in Australia yet, so it'll be some time before we take on the rest of the planet. Probably it'll be up to the next generation to carry on our work." She added with a mischievous smile, "For example, I must say I've been impressed by David's interest in environmental issues."

It was a relief to have Aunt Sarah tease her in the customary way. Carol said with mock anger, "So now you're leading my son astray! I demand you keep him safe from those crones of yours."

David adored Aunt Sarah, who'd been a surrogate grandmother to him. Even now that he was older, with the usual teenage life filled with school, sport and socializing, he was always keen to see her. Carol thought with a pang how often she'd been relieved that Aunt Sarah could stand in for her when the demands of Carol's job had unexpectedly intruded into the time set aside to spend with David.

In an unspoken agreement, the meal continued with lighthearted banter. Carol was sure none of them could put the real situation out of mind. Sybil had left her car back at Carol's, so the three of them continued chatting as Carol drove home. To Carol's guilty relief, Sybil made it clear she was tired, and wouldn't be coming into the house.

As soon as Carol parked, Aunt Sarah leapt out. "I'll see you inside, Carol. Sybil, dear, I'll talk with you tomorrow."

Carol felt a stab of anger, positive her aunt had deliberately set it up so she'd be alone with Sybil. "I'll walk you to your car," she said.

"It's awkward, isn't it?" said Sybil as they reached her vehicle.

"What do you mean?"

"I mean us — or rather, the fact that we're not *us*."

Carol shrugged, not wanting to put into words what she might, or might not be feeling. In fact, she realized, she felt detached, cool.

"I know about Leota Woolfe."

Carol gave a gasp of exasperation. "I suppose Aunt Sarah told you, did she?"

"No, actually it was Pat."

Moving from exasperation to anger, Carol snapped, "Great! You and Mark and Pat have all been discussing me, have you?"

"No, of course we haven't," said Sybil. "It just came up in conversation."

Carol glowered at her, but knew she was being unfair. A couple of months ago Carol had come out of a meeting to find Leota and Bourke chatting like old friends. Leota had unexpectedly been in Sydney for the day, and had called by the Police Center to say hello. "I've been telling Mark all about how we met," she had said cheerfully, "and how you lured me to Australia."

Afterwards, when they had been alone in Carol's office, Carol had said coldly, "Why did you tell Mark about us? I would never do that."

Her face showing her astonishment, Leota had protested, "But our relationship isn't a secret, honey. You're not in the closet, and besides, you've talked about Mark Bourke often, so I knew you were close friends. That's true, isn't it?"

"Yes, we are, but I prefer to keep some things off-limits." When Leota had seemed baffled, Carol had added, "I feel strongly about personal privacy. It's just the way I am."

Afterwards she hadn't said a word about it to Bourke. He, in his usual easy-going way, had taken a lead from Carol and hadn't referred to his conversation with Leota either. Of course he would have mentioned it to his wife, Pat.

"I'm sorry," she said to Sybil. "I'm over-reacting."

"I often see Pat. We're friends, and she thought I'd like to know. And she was right. It makes it easier for me to tell you that I'm seeing someone too."

"It's nothing to do with me who you see."

Sybil sighed. "Okay, Carol. Goodnight."

She got into her car, put down the window, and said, "About Aunt Sarah, I can take time off from work, even at short notice. Just let me know what's happening, please."

"Is it someone I know?"

Sybil shook her head. "No."

"Serious?"

Sybil's lips curved. "I believe you said it was nothing to do with you."

"Just curious."

"I'm not sure. Maybe."

Carol watched her drive off, then stalked back inside. Her aunt was sitting in the kitchen, a guileless expression on her face. "I thought you might like another coffee, and I think I've solved the mysteries of your percolator."

"Okay, aunt, you deliberately left us alone out there."

"I thought it was about time you two had a sensible conversation together."

"Right. We've had it, okay." Her aunt opened her mouth, but before she could speak Carol snapped, "No, I'm not discussing it, so don't ask."

Ten silent minutes later they were both sitting at the kitchen bench with mugs of coffee. Finally Carol said, "To change the subject completely, do you happen to know anything about a death at Govetts Leap last year? A man out jogging was killed when he fell from the lookout while his wife was in a car nearby."

Aunt Sarah's expression darkened. "That'd be Barry Lyne. Why are you interested?"

"I don't know if I am, yet. There may be some connection to another case."

"If it's anything underhand, Lyne is likely to be involved."

There was so much antipathy in her voice that Carol looked at her with surprise. "I get the distinct feeling you didn't like him."

"I never met the man, but he was pushing the development of a big tourist resort that was going to flout Blue Mountain environmental laws right, left and center."

"So he was a controversial figure in the district?"

"Too right. My Eco-Crones were up in arms."

Resigned to the answer she knew was coming, Carol said, "You and your group demonstrated, I suppose?"

"We certainly did," said Aunt Sarah with satisfaction. "Several times. Eco-Crones for the Environment made the local news in a big way. Next time you're up, I'll show you our scrapbook. Of course, as I said before, soon you'll be able to log on and see everything on our website."

Enthusiasm had filled Aunt Sarah's face. Carol could see she was in for a detailed account of the latest exploits of her aunt's environmental group.

Carol said hastily, "Can we concentrate on Mr. Lyne for the moment?"

"If you insist, although he's hardly worth spending too much time on. If you believed all Lyne said, you'd think he was single-handedly going to reinvigorate the whole Blue Mountains economy. Basically a slick con-artist, out to make money, no matter what damage he did. There was quite a to-do in the district when he died. And lots of gossip about his wife, Alyce."

"I gather that at the time he fell, she was parked in their car, waiting for him to finish his run."

Aunt Sarah nodded slowly, her mouth pursed. "That's what she said, Carol, but there was plenty of talk that she, or maybe her lover, blipped her husband over the edge."

"A lover?"

"The general consensus was that she was having it off with a local cop" — she waved her hand dismissively — "but that was just talk."

"The local cop wouldn't have been Chief Inspector Block, would it?"

"Saul Block?" said Aunt Sarah with scorn. "Have you seen

50

the man? *Most* unattractive. It's not him, if only for the fact that his wife, Ida, would skin him alive if he stepped out of line. No, it was supposed to be someone lower in the ranks. There were plenty of fingers pointed, but no name ever came up. There was even some suggestion Alyce Lyne's brother had something to do with her husband's death."

"You certainly live in the fast lane in the mountains," Carol observed.

Her aunt took this as a compliment. "You could say that, although it's the same as anywhere — only of course, more beautiful."

"Tell me about the brother."

Aunt Sarah shrugged. "I don't know much to tell. I'm not even sure if I can remember his name — it's Ian something-or-other. Anyway, he's younger than his sister, late twenties, I'd say, and very protective. After the accident, every photo you saw of her, he was there."

"Is Alyce Lyne still living in the area?"

"I heard she moved away, but where to I don't know." Aunt Sarah dusted off her hands, obviously done with the subject. "That's it, Carol. It's a pity someone died, but some good came out of it. With Barry Lyne gone, the financing on his horrible development fell through, which means many plants and animals have been saved from certain destruction."

"Good," said Carol absently.

"Oh, for heaven's sake, Carol! If it's that important to you I'll put you in touch with Lillian Broadhall. She's a founding member of the Eco-Crones and she knows everything about everybody. She'll have the all the dirt for you, if you want it."

"Thank you. That would be great."

Aunt Sarah looked at her narrowly. "Don't you ever get tired of it? The gossip and insinuations and scandal-mongering? How people love to say something bad about someone else?"

"It's my job to investigate. That means I listen to what people have to say."

"Erk," said Aunt Sarah. "I'd hate it, dealing with all that garbage."

"It isn't all garbage, aunt. It's often evidence of a particular crime, where what people see and hear can prove someone guilty, or innocent."

Aunt Sarah made an indeterminate noise that nevertheless conveyed her disapproval.

"I don't suppose," said Carol innocently, "that your Eco-Crones ever gossip — or do they?"

"Never," said Aunt Sarah with dignity. She added with a reluctant smile. "We *discuss,* at length. That's all."

CHAPTER SIX

The clinic was an anonymous medical building with clean lines and an antiseptic lobby. Carol felt uncomfortably on edge, but Aunt Sarah seemed reasonably relaxed, her tension only showing in her uncharacteristic silence and the tight grip with which she clutched the envelope containing the mammograms and written report from the radiologist in the Blue Mountains.

When she was whisked away by a sweetly-smiling young woman in a pale blue uniform, Carol tried to get into the paperback she'd been meaning to start for some time. Highly recommended by literary critics, it was a family drama that was full of suffering and tragedy. By the time the fourth catastrophe had struck the unfortunate family within the first few chapters, Carol had had enough, thinking that if she'd been a depressive, she'd be positively suicidal by now.

After checking with the receptionist that her aunt would be some time longer, Carol strolled out the front door of the center in search of something lighter to read. It was a beautiful autumn day, crisp but not cold. She found a sheltered spot and called Bourke on her mobile phone. Assured nothing of any interest had occurred, she rang off and sauntered in the direction of the shop she'd noticed earlier when driving along the street.

Inside she found a rack of books, and was checking through them when her phone rang. A double homicide had just been called in. She scribbled down the address, told Bourke she'd meet him at the crime scene as soon as she could, and walked briskly back to the clinic.

Her timing was perfect. Aunt Sarah emerged on the arm of the young woman who had taken her away. Looking rather pale, but resolute, her aunt announced the procedure for the needle biopsy had been rather unexpected.

Carol sat her down in one of the chairs in the waiting room. "You mean it hurt you?" she asked with concern.

"No, not really, because I had a local anesthetic," said Aunt Sarah. "But I had to lie on my stomach on a table that had a hole in it so my boob could hang through while they took a set of mammograms to pinpoint the tumor on a screen. I was told not to move, but the team who did the biopsy kept up a stream of comments that made me laugh, so keeping still was rather hard. Anyway, once they established where the lump was, they guided the needle in and took a sample." She patted her left breast very gently. "Got an ice pack in my bra."

Carol asked, "When will we know?"

"Dr. Wu wants me back here on Monday afternoon to get the results. I can get a taxi —"

"No way. I'll drive you."

"That's wonderful, because Dr. Wu wants you to sit in on the consultation, you being my closest living relative."

This sounded ominous to Carol. Had the doctor already decided it was likely to be upsetting news? "Did this doctor say anything about the lump?"

"Well, I know I've got it in the most common site, the upper part of the breast near the armpit, and if it is cancer, she thinks it's early stage."

Last night, after her aunt had gone to bed, Carol had logged onto the Internet and researched breast cancer. She was rapidly becoming familiar with terms she'd never bothered about before, such as ductal carcinoma, lobular carcinoma, medullary, tubular and mucinous carcinoma. She'd also checked through the treatments, not having fully realized before how much the regimen was tailored to each patient's particular needs.

"You wait here. I'll get the car and pick you up in front of the building."

The fact Aunt Sarah didn't argue was significant. When she climbed into the front seat she flinched, and Carol felt a stab of remorse as she said, "Aunt, I'm afraid I've had a call from work. Would you be all right alone at home? Shall I call Sybil? She said she'd be available at short notice."

"I don't need babysitting. I'm tired — I didn't sleep well — so I think I'll lie down." She gave Carol a small smile. "And did you booknote the sites on cancer you were looking at last night? I'd like to take a glance at them myself."

"I'll give you my password."

"No need," said Aunt Sarah. "You're not the only detective in the family. I already know it."

"I hate these murder-suicides," said Bourke, wrinkling his nose. He looked moodily at the two bodies sprawled on the pale tiles of the kitchen floor. "Although thank God there are no kids involved. It's even worse then."

"You're not wrong." Carol had seen enough of the sickening violence desperate parents could do to their children. Of necessity she was very familiar with murder. When the victims were babies or youngsters who had every reason to believe their parents would take care of them, the carnage was particularly upsetting, even for hardened professionals.

The deceased had been identified: Joseph and Faye McDonald. Both in their early thirties, childless, apparently healthy, and from the outside view probably appearing to have everything to live for and nothing to justify this bloody scene of carnage that had ended their lives. The house was in an up-scale neighborhood, the garage held a new Mercedes and a BMW, the furnishings had that well-bred elegance that money and good taste achieve. The kitchen itself was magazine-photo perfect, except for the evidence of slaughter.

Having come late to the crime scene, Carol had missed seeing the police doctor. Liz Carey had also left after setting her team to work.

"Who found the bodies, Mark?"

"Faye McDonald's sister. She's in the front room with Anne at the moment."

"You've spoken with her?"

"Just a few words. I thought you'd like to see her yourself. Either she's very much under control, or she's a cold fish who isn't all that much thrown by what she's found."

The metallic smell of blood was in Carol's nostrils. Both bodies had sustained headshots. Blood and tissue had splattered on white surfaces and collected in congealing pools around the shattered skulls. "You sure it's a murder-suicide?"

"Classic," said Bourke. "The husband confronts his wife here in the kitchen, shotgun in hand. Maybe he just walks in and fires, or maybe he tells her why she's got to die and they argue, but whichever, the result's the same — half her head is blown away. He looks at what he's done, turns the shotgun on himself and fires the other barrel. Bam! She's dead, he's dead. End of story."

"The coroner may require a little more than that at the inquest."

Bourke grinned at Carol's dry tone. "Of course we'll go through all the motions, but in the end it'll be decided that this guy totally lost it, killed his wife and then himself. Although . . ."

"Although what?"

"Take a close look at the guy." Carol bent over the corpse, repressing a wince. She'd seen many victims who'd died brutal deaths, but she always found close-range shotgun blasts particularly gruesome.

Pointing, Bourke said, "You know as well as I do that the majority of people planning a shotgun suicide place the barrel under the chin before they pull the trigger, so that the blast goes through the roof of the mouth and up into the brain. This guy blew most of his face off. The angle of the blast started at about level with his nostrils and exited high at the back of his head."

"Where's the weapon?"

"Liz took it with her to drop off at the lab. It was a standard side-by-side double-barreled shotgun. Nothing fancy."

Visualizing the suicide, Carol said, "With the length of the barrel, it would be difficult to hold a shotgun that way and fire it at the same time. That's why so many people prop the butt of the gun on the floor — it's easy to reach down and pull the trigger."

"Difficult to do, but not impossible," said Bourke.

The face of the dead man was all but destroyed. Carol said, "Is there any doubt it's the husband?"

"His sister-in-law says it's him."

"Inspector Ashton," called one of the crime scene technicians. "You'll want to see this."

Followed by Bourke, Carol took the long route around the bodies to avoid contaminating the area. "What is it?"

The technician, a young, solemn-faced man named Urban,

indicated the torn piece of paper that he carefully held in tweezers. "Spotted it against the base of the stove."

Carol squinted at the words not obliterated by blood. "Printout of an e-mail?"

"Looks like it." He turned it so Carol could see more clearly. *Darling, darling Faye, please don't tell him anything about us just say you're leav . . .*

Bourke spread his hands. "I told you, Carol. Open and shut case."

"Maybe too open and shut."

The murder victim's sister was slightly-built and looked to be in her early forties. She sat rigidly on a cream leather sofa, her feet flat on the floor and her hands folded neatly in her lap. Carol evaluated her quickly. The woman had waxen skin, pale, dull hair and wore a brown skirt and plain, beige blouse. Her only adornment was a watch and a chased silver ring on the little finger of her right hand.

A colorless woman, Carol was thinking, when Penelope Neale looked up for a moment, and Carol caught a flash of eyes of vivid blue before she returned her gaze to the richly-patterned rug on the floor. Carol's initial impression dissolved. It wasn't the contrast of the woman's startling eyes alone, but an almost palpable sense of calculation, of a mind assessing and adjusting for the situation.

"I'm Detective Inspector Carol Ashton, Ms Neale. I'm sorry to have to ask you questions at this time, but I hope you'll understand the necessity."

She shot Carol another glance, then looked back at the floor again. "Of course, Inspector. Anything I can do to help. It's all been such a terrible shock. I can't believe Faye's gone."

There was so little emotion in her tone that her words might well have been spoken by a synthesized voice.

"Will you excuse me for a moment," said Carol, beckoning Anne Newsome to follow her out into the hallway. Once there, Carol asked, "Has she said anything while you've been sitting with her?"

"Quite a lot, actually. Gave me a run-down of her sister's situation, saying that she alone was the person who knew the grief the husband was causing her sister. To quote Ms. Neale, 'It was a perfect marriage on the outside, but hell on the inside.'"

"Does she seem genuinely upset to you?"

Anne tilted her dark head, considering. "I'd have to say no, but you know how shock takes some people. She could be holding it together by sheer will and fall apart any minute now."

Wide experience with next of kin had convinced Carol that the reactions to sudden death, particularly violent death, varied widely. Even so, she had a feeling Penelope Neale was not likely to break down, unless it happened to be a carefully calculated performance.

"Have you got a gut feeling about her?"

Anne grinned, clearly pleased to be asked her opinion. "Don't quote me, but I think she's bunging on an act."

After sending Anne to relieve Mark Bourke, who was organizing a house-to-house to ascertain if anyone had heard or seen anything, Carol went back into the room. It seemed to her that Penelope Neale hadn't moved at all. She still sat to attention, her blue eyes fixed on a point on the floor in front of her feet.

"You found your sister and her husband?"

"Yes. I was at the office, early like I always am, and when neither of them came in by about nine o'clock I got worried. I asked my secretary to call the house, but there was no answer, so I put my appointments on hold and came around. And I found..." She put her face in her hands. "It was horrible."

59

Carol would have felt more sympathy if she hadn't caught the quick assessing glance Penelope Neale sent her before she hid her face.

"Did your brother-in-law own a shotgun?"

"I believe so. He hunted ducks, I think, but I'm not totally sure." She screwed up her face. "I hate guns."

Mark Bourke came in to the room. "We've got something — a neighbor down the street who heard the shots."

Penelope Neale looked up. "When?"

"What time did you get here, Ms. Neale?"

The woman's blue eyes narrowed. "You don't think I had anything to do with this, Inspector? That's outrageous."

"Not at all," said Carol smoothly. "We merely need to establish a timeline."

"I'm not exactly sure of the time I arrived. Around ten, ten-thirty. Surely my call to the police was logged."

Bourke said mildly, "You may not have called immediately."

"I did. And when I arrived at the house, I spoke to someone before I came inside. A retired man, next door. Then I went down the side of the house to the back — that's what I always do, come in through the kitchen — and I found . . ." She put her head down again. "This is very hard," she whispered.

Carol and Bourke exchanged glances. "Nine o'clock," he mouthed. Carol nodded, then looked at the woman's bowed head. *You're not quite convincing enough*, she thought.

She could see from Mark Bourke's expression that he too was wondering why Penelope Neale was going out of her way to make sure they knew she'd definitely arrived long after the event.

Bourke said, "Were you aware your sister was having an affair?"

His question seemed to startle her. "I'm sorry?" she said.

"I asked if you were aware that your sister was having an affair."

"I knew there was someone . . ." She raised one hand in a helpless gesture. "I wish I could be more help, Inspector, but Faye never told me his name. All I know is that he was important to her."

She dabbed at her eyes with a tissue. Carol could swear they were dry of tears. Carol said bluntly, "You have no idea of his identity? I find that hard to believe."

Indignation swept across Penelope Neale's plain face. "I had no inkling. How could I, if Faye didn't confide in me?"

"But you knew there was serious trouble in the marriage."

"Of course I did. To most people it must have seemed an ideal match, but I've seen myself how difficult Joseph can be in private." She shook her head. "Still, the idea he might do something so violent . . ." A sigh. "Frankly, it never occurred to me."

"We may have further questions," said Carol, "so I must ask you to stay here for a few minutes more, Ms. Neale."

"Very well, but I need to get back to the office."

Outside the room and out of earshot down the hall, Carol said to Bourke, "What do you think?"

"She's trying too hard."

"I agree."

"Of course," said Bourke, grinning, "In her place I think I'd try even harder."

Carol raised her eyebrows. "A motive?"

"You could say that. The neighbors were very helpful with information. It seems that the three of them, Penelope Neale, her sister and her brother-in-law, are equal partners in a video game company, small, but wildly successful, and a candidate for a takeover by a larger firm. Now that her partners are dead, it all goes to Penelope. I call that a substantial motive"

"And did she speak to a neighbor when she arrived?"

"Oh, yes," said Bourke. "Mr. Havisham, a retired gentleman who lives next door. He was working in his front garden when she parked her car and came over to him. Mr. Havisham had met Penelope Neale before, but she introduced herself again, said she was worried about her sister because she'd failed to arrive at work, and specifically asked if he had heard anything."

"Had he?"

"He told her he hadn't," said Bourke.

"Two shotgun blasts? That's quite a noise. I'm surprised he didn't notice."

"When I interviewed Mr. Havisham I found that he was rather deaf, and a bit defensive about it, so I gather he doesn't use his hearing aid all that much."

"That's great," said Carol with a grimace. "What's his eyesight like?"

"Seems to be fine, but he didn't see anything either. No one coming or going that he noticed. The interesting thing is, however, he did mention that Ms. Neale made quite a business about exactly what time it was, checking her watch with his to verify it was ten past ten."

"It almost looks as though she were trying to establish an alibi."

Bourke screwed up his face. "Isn't a murder-suicide complicated enough for you?" he asked facetiously. "Now you're suggesting just what?"

"I'm thinking murder for hire," said Carol, matching his light-hearted tone.

She wasn't altogether joking. Penelope Neale's attitude and behavior had set off in Carol the small, insistent alarm she'd learned to trust.

CHAPTER SEVEN

Friday morning Carol checked her action list and mentally groaned at Terry Roham's name. Not because Terry had come to her with a complaint to be resolved, but because of the time it would take out of her day. The deaths of Joseph and Faye McDonald had put yet another case on her schedule.

She smiled wryly, remembering Mark Bourke's facetious comment two days earlier that bodies were stacking up in the hallway of the morgue awaiting post mortems. If the rate violent deaths were occurring was maintained, the morgue would soon be hiring refrigerated vans to take the overflow.

Liz Carey had left a message that the fingerprints found on the safety fence at the site of Trelawney's fall at North Head had not been matched with any person in the data bank, nor with Trelawney himself. Carol made a note in the file, thinking with irritation she'd have to chase up Richie Dent at Manly Station for his report before she could prepare her own for the coroner.

A call from Leota put her in a much better frame of mind. "Saturday night? I believe I'm available," Carol said, "although perhaps I should check my busy social calendar."

"Please do," said Leota with a chuckle. "I would appreciate your company, although I can move on to my second choice."

"Which is?"

"Television and a bag of potato chips."

"Clearly it's my duty to save you from that. What time will you be free?"

"Six o'clock should do it. Will you come here to the hotel, or shall I come to you?"

"My Aunt Sarah's staying with me at the moment." Carol hesitated, then added, "She's down from the mountains for some medical tests."

"I'd love to meet her. You've been promising we will for some time now."

Last night Aunt Sarah had almost been her normal bouncy self, but Carol wasn't sure she'd welcome socializing with a stranger when there was so much on her mind.

"I'm sorry, Leota, but I'll have to let you know about whether or not Aunt Sarah's available, but in any case, I guarantee I'll be there to pick you up at your hotel at six tomorrow."

She smiled as she disconnected. The weekend seemed suddenly full of promise. Her pleasure faded a little as she thought of the conversation with Sybil the night before, and how incensed she'd been to discover Sybil had been discussing Leota Woolfe with Pat. Carol wasn't ashamed of her relationship with Leota, so why did she have this knee-jerk reaction as soon as she realized people had been discussing them?

There's nothing wrong, she reasoned, with maintaining reticence about her personal self. It often amazed Carol how some individuals would discuss without hesitation the most intimate details of their lives, sometimes with people who were virtual strangers. She could never imagine doing that.

She decided to talk with Bourke about Terry Roham before Renfrew Downing arrived to see her. He'd called that morning to make an appointment. She's always been fond of Ren, and was looking forward the meeting. She had no idea why he'd called it, but was convinced it had nothing to do with Ren headhunting her for Downing & Pate, no matter what Mark Bourke surmised.

She glanced through Terry Roham's personnel file, finding nothing of note, then called Bourke into her office.

"Shut the door, please," she said when he entered.

Bourke looked askance, but didn't comment, simply closing the door and taking a seat near her desk. He said, "Captain Trelawney's post mortem is scheduled for Monday afternoon."

Aunt Sarah's appointment with Dr. Wu was on Monday afternoon, and Carol wanted to be there. "Mark, I hate to ask a favor, but —"

"You want me to attend? Okay," he said agreeably, making Carol feel unfair to be raising the next topic. Bourke had been so easy-going about something Carol herself should be doing.

It was best to come right to the point. "Terry Roham's made a complaint. Apparently it's his perception that Anne is being allocated the most interesting jobs, and he's getting the dregs."

She passed the list of incidents Terry had compiled over the desk. Bourke frowned at it, then flung it down.

"So Terry thinks I'm favoring Anne?"

"It seems so. What's your take on it?"

Bourke sat forward, leaning his elbows on his knees. "Ah, Jesus," he said.

With his good-natured personality, Carol had expected perhaps a response of irritation from Bourke, but not anger. She was surprised to realize he was furious.

"Look, Carol, Anne is just about as good as you get. She's efficient, takes initiative where it's appropriate, and always makes sure I know what's going on. Why wouldn't I give her challenging tasks? She gets things done, and I can rely on what she tells me."

"And Terry?"

"Terry Roham? It's my fault there's a problem. I've been too busy to take the time to keep a strict eye on him, so I'm afraid I've tended to bypass Terry if the task is likely to be challenging, and give it to someone I don't have to supervise closely."

This was a situation Carol could not have visualized. For years Mark Bourke had been her steady, absolutely reliable second-in-command. "Bloody hell, Mark, why didn't you tell me you had problems with Terry before he came directly to me with accusations of favoritism?"

Bourke ran a hand over his face. "Believe me, I'm kicking myself over this, but you know how it is — these young constables come in wet behind the ears. Some of them will more than make the grade, but most of them are just average. The real no-hopers drop out sooner rather than later, but guys like Terry Roham are keen, and stick around. They're the sort that need guidance and an occasional good kick up the backside, but frankly, I took the easy way out and gave the more difficult tasks to others, particularly Anne."

"Did you point out to him the times when you considered his work wasn't up to standard?"

"A comment maybe, but nothing formal."

Carol couldn't believe she'd been so slack. This problem had obviously been simmering for some time, and yet she hadn't picked up on it. It was, she silently berated herself, her failure, more than Bourke's. She'd come to rely on him so much that she'd taken for granted everything under his control was going smoothly.

"What about his evaluations?" She indicated Roham's personnel file. "They're not excellent, but they're okay."

Bourke looked both embarrassed and contrite. "I'm sorry, Carol. It's easier to be non-committal than have something blow up in your face. I take full responsibility."

"I told Terry I'd raise the matter with you, and then the three of us would have a meeting."

Bourke's homely face was set in determined lines. "I created this mess, so let me have a go at resolving it before you get further involved. I'll take Roham out for a beer after work, and see if we can settle the matter between us."

"That sounds like a good idea, but I still want the three of us to have a meeting."

He nodded agreement, but wasn't happy about it. "It's a bit of a storm in a teacup," he said. "I mean, think of when you and I were young cops. We got the shit jobs then, as a matter of course."

"I believe," said Carol with a trace of acid in her voice, "that Constable Roham has a valid complaint that more than his fair share of shit has been coming his way."

Bourke nodded, his manner subdued. He stood, said, "I'll get back to you," and without meeting her eyes, left her office.

"Carol!" The man at her door advanced, arms wide. Carol came from behind her desk to hug him.

"Ren Downing. I haven't seen you for ages. How's the private eye business these days?"

"Can't complain. Lots of insurance work, and with threats of terrorism on the rise, there's a big demand for personal and corporate safety consulting. I'm flat to the boards and so is Gemma, but we're raking in the dollars. And we've actually got staff! Can you imagine it, me a boss, with a personal assistant, and underlings?"

"Only with great difficulty," said Carol, waving him to a seat. She went back behind the protection of her desk, wondering as she did so why she hadn't taken the chair beside him. They were good friends, after all, even if she hadn't spoken with him for some time.

As she sat down the reason for her action became clear to her, and she smiled. Although she'd discounted completely Bourke's idea that Ren Downing was there to offer her a position at Downing & Pate, she'd unconsciously put the desk between them, just in case that was his purpose in seeing her. This position put her in charge of the room, and made him the petitioner.

"You're smiling, Carol. You must be pleased to see me."

"You know I always am."

She regarded her visitor with curiosity. Ren hadn't changed much, still the tall, lanky individual with whom she'd spent much of her early career. His dark hair was now flecked with gray. Apart from a spray of laugh lines at the corners of his dark eyes, his gaunt, intelligent face with its long nose and mobile mouth was still the same. He'd always dressed well, and today had on a dark suit of impeccable cut, a white shirt, and red silk tie. As he unbuttoned his jacket she caught a flash of red lining, exactly matching the shade of his tie.

Her close inspection amused him. "Do I past muster, Carol? I must say you defy time and remain the gorgeous, green-eyed blonde I remember so fondly."

"I was thinking how outstandingly handsome you are. And with such good dress sense . . ."

Her mocking tone made him laugh. "Let's just agree that we're both almost too good looking to live."

"Would you like coffee?"

"No way, babe," he said with a grin. "I've had too much police brew in my day. These days I only drink the good stuff."

"Babe?"

"Tough talk, Carol. We private eyes use it all the time. Part of the image. I've been picking up my vocab from Raymond Chandler and the like."

"That should impress clients."

"Well, I'm judicious where I use it. I don't try to dazzle a bank or a big insurance company. With them I assume my low-key, ultra-professional demeanor. You'd laugh to see me."

Carol looked at him with affection. "It's been much too long. We really should get together, soon."

"Great idea. Ben will be keen."

Remembering that the last time she'd been out in a foursome with Ren Downing and his significant other of many years, she'd been with Sybil, Carol said, "Ren, I'm not —"

"With Sybil anymore? Naturally I'm privy to that information. I'm a private eye, for God's sake, so I know everything."

"I hope not."

Downing chuckled. "I exaggerate, as always. So I have no idea if you have anyone special in your life. Have you?"

"Maybe." Before he could press her for details, she went on, "Ren, I don't want to rush you, but . . ."

"I know you're busy. I'll get to the point, although it's going to sound a bit melodramatic. It's to do with some cases we've been investigating for various insurance companies. I'm sure you already know that when there's a considerable payout on a policy, insurance executives like it checked out, and that's where Downing and Pate come in."

"No doubt you're looking for insurance fraud."

"Absolutely. And distressingly, human nature being what it is, there's more than enough fraud to find. For example, workers' compensation brings out the worst in people — you'd be astonished at how many bogus claims there are for crippling back injuries that magically disappear when the supposed victims don't think they're being observed."

"This is all very interesting, but —"

"You're wondering why in the hell I've popped in, out of the blue, to tell you all this."

"Enlighten me."

"Okay, a bit of background first. We investigate insurance

claims statewide, not just in the metropolitan area of Sydney, and because we work for several different insurance bodies, sometimes we can pick up a pattern that wouldn't be obvious to anyone else. Companies covering vehicle insurance share information, so, for example, staged accidents and the resulting dodgy medical claims get noticed, even when the con artists move their operations from city to city. It's the same with suspicious fires, because an arsonist often repeats the crime, so it's worthwhile to look for similarities."

"Life insurance?" said Carol.

"Ah," said Ren, "I always knew you weren't just a pretty face. Life insurance is exactly the area my concern. We've been noticing a repetition of characteristics that are rather alarming . . . Well, they alarm me."

"Would accidental death, perhaps caused by falling from a great height, be included in this pattern you mention?"

Ren looked at her with deep approval. "Very good! So you've picked it up, too."

"I haven't actually picked anything up, so I can't take any credit. It's nothing concrete, at least not yet, but there have been a couple of cases where accidental death was the finding at the time, but now we're thinking it may be worthwhile looking at them again."

Downing pursed his lips. "Only a couple?" he said.

"How many have you got?"

"Four deaths ruled accidents that I consider definitely suspicious, and a fifth that could be on the list."

"A possible five murders?" said Carol, unpleasantly surprised. She remembered Mark Bourke saying to her that if the total of doubtful accidents reached four, she'd have to admit something was going on. Now here was Ren with five. "How sure are you they're not genuine accidents?" she asked.

"I'm pretty well convinced, but I have to point out I could be wrong about one or more of them. You know how it is when you start looking for criminal intent — you see it everywhere. I'm more than willing to grant sometimes I may be seeing murder when, in fact, it's nothing more than carelessness or stupidity on the part of the deceased."

Carol took the top off her gold pen. "Give me details."

"Okay, what I first noticed were coincidences. The same scenario occurs several times: the victim, usually a spouse, has recently taken out a life insurance policy, or alternatively, the coverage of an existing policy has been considerably increased. Shortly thereafter, a fatal accident eliminates the insured, either a fall that no one witnesses, or a hit-and-run where a stolen car is found, but there's no evidence to link anyone to the crime. In each instance, the beneficiary of the policy has a firm alibi for exactly the right time."

"Sheer luck?" asked Carol. "Coincidences do happen, Ren."

"Alibis are slippery things, as you know. People just don't pay close attention to time, for example, unless it's pointed out to them. It just so happens in each of these cases the beneficiary managed to find a way to make sure a witness would collaborate the fact that an airtight alibi existed."

"I have trouble visualizing Murder Incorporated out in the suburbs," said Carol, her tone light, although the ramifications of what Ren Downing was saying had hollowed her stomach.

"It's a sure-fire scheme. You get rid of an inconvenient spouse or business partner, the inquest finds accidental death, the insurance company obligingly makes you rich."

Matching his flippancy, Carol said, "There's a murder co-ordinator somewhere? Maybe there's a website covering murder for fun and profit?"

"Carol, there's a real possibility that there's an entre-preneur who is" — Ren Downing paused for a wicked smile — "making a killing out there."

"You're serious?"

He sobered. "I'm serious when I say some, or even all of them that fall into this pattern could be murders. And re-member, I only have information on deaths where the deceased was insured by one of the insurance companies that use Downing and Pate. Who knows how many other accidental murders there may be that we know nothing about?"

"Has an insurance company refused to pay up because they agreed with you that the claim was suspicious?"

He turned his mouth down in mock dejection. "The buggers have paid them all."

"So they didn't find the claims suspicious?"

"Fair go, Carol. At first neither did I, or Gemma. It was only after we compared notes that we picked up that something odd was going on, and by that time the first three policies had been paid out. Then, although we waved a red flag in our report on the last death, the insurance company didn't find convincing enough reasons to hold up payment, especially as the cops didn't find anything questionable."

"Names and places, Ren."

Carol wrote down the cases as Ren Downing ran through them. When he'd finished, she put her chin on her hand and read through her notes: Barry Lyne, killed by a two-hundred meter fall at Blackheath, Blue Mountains; Wayne Cronnite, victim of a fatal hit-and-run in Newcastle; Cindy Dunn, died of head injuries after a fall down fire stairs in a Sydney office block; Hildy Perry, drowned in heavy seas at Kiama, South Coast, after falling from a headland. There were three insurance companies involved: Australasian Risk, Callard Insurance and International Fire, Flood and Life.

"Are your two in there?" Ren asked.

"The first one is — Barry Lyne at Govetts Leap in the Blue Mountains. You haven't got the second, a Paulette Bruehl from Wollongong, who died last year when she fell at the Gap, Watson's Bay."

As he wrote down the name, Carol said, "You said there was a fifth case you weren't sure about."

"Yes, a woman called Ursula Stein who lived out west in Dubbo. Everything else fits the overall pattern — the recent large policy on her life, the fact that her husband came up with a firm alibi for just the required time period — but she died from carbon monoxide poisoning. Carelessly left her car running inside a closed garage. At the inquest it was ruled an accident because there was no evidence of suicide, plus her husband testified that she was notoriously thoughtless, and had nearly been overcome before in a similar incident. Callard Insurance paid up without a squeak."

"I'm really hoping you're wrong about all this, Ren."

"Me too. By the way, I saw in the news someone went over North Head a couple of days ago. Lately, every time I hear someone has fallen from a great height I'm swept with paranoia. Anything suss about this one?"

"Not so far. We'll have the post mortem results Monday afternoon. The victim's wife was at North Head in a parked car at the time, but she didn't make any efforts to find a witness to establish where she was and when, so that doesn't fit your pattern."

Ren grinned. *"My* pattern?" In an exaggerated American accent, he added, "Finely-honed private eye skills are telling me that it'll be *your* pattern soon, my little honeybun."

"Oh, please, not honeybun," said Carol. "I'd almost rather babe."

Ren leapt to his feet, slapped down a cream-colored, embossed business card in front of Carol, and stood back. "I trust you'll be in touch, so here's my card, babe."

Examining it, she said, "What? No magnifying glass or deerstalker hat?"

"Please! We're a well-established, discreet organization. Nothing flashy."

"Except for you, Ren."

"Except for me," he agreed.

CHAPTER EIGHT

"Did Ren Downing offer you a job?"

Carol looked up from the file she was reading on Paulette Bruehl's fatal fall at the Gap. "No, Mark, and Ren didn't look as if the thought had ever crossed his mind. I'm sorry I didn't have a bet with you over it — I would have cleaned up."

"For once I'm pleased to be wrong."

She sat back to study him. "You didn't really think I'd jump ship, did you?"

He shrugged. "I thought you might be tempted."

"Never," she said, thinking that maybe, just maybe, at some future time she could visualize herself working somewhere else other than the Police Service.

Bourke appeared to have regained his good humor. "I've

lined Terry Roham up for a drink at the pub after work. We'll straighten things out between us, I'm sure."

"Boys bonding over beer on a Friday night," said Carol with a sardonic curl to her lip. "When I was a young constable it was still the time when females, if they wanted any credibility, had to behave like honorary blokes and toss back the beers at the local watering hole. Career-wise, you got nowhere, unless you joined in. Those were the days." Her tone made it clear she didn't miss them in the slightest.

The hint of apprehension on his face made her chuckle. "Relax, Mark. I'm not about to launch into a tirade about the treatment of women in the Police Service. What I am going to do is tell you why Ren Downing came to see me."

As she recounted her conversation with Downing she watched Bourke's expression reflect first interest, then surprise, and lastly consternation. "Bloody hell," he said, "when I raised the idea that investigation of a couple of accidental falls might show them to be something more sinister, I had no idea there was a virtual epidemic of murder-accidents out there."

"We don't know that there is, yet."

"I've always said the best way to get away with murder is to make it look like an accident."

Carol sent him a long-suffering look. "Not altogether an original thought, Mark. In fact I read that an eminent English mystery writer, when asked how she would kill someone, recommended a quick push over a cliff as being an excellent method that held little fear of arrest."

"Now I'm really interested in the results of the Trelawney post mortem on Monday," said Bourke. "Given that the guy fell so far, it'd a chance in a million to find anything unusual, but if something's there, Jeff Duke's the one to find it."

Carol nodded her agreement. Jeff Duke was the best forensic pathologist she'd known. He was bluff and hearty, but not unfeeling, and seemed to have a sixth sense where cause of death was concerned. Attending post mortems was part of

Carol's job, but she couldn't imagine facing death in all its manifestations day after day the way the pathologist did. Especially children. The death of innocents always hit Carol hard, however matter-of-fact she appeared on the surface.

Even Jeff Duke was subdued on such occasions. She'd seen his big hands cradle a deceased baby's head, gazing down at the little, still face as though there was some silent communication between the two of them. Then he'd point out almost imperceptible signs that indicated how death had occurred, and further examination of the body, or later lab results, would confirm his findings.

Pushing such images aside, she went to remind Bourke that he was to call her on Monday as soon as he had the preliminary results of John Trelawney's post mortem. Deep in thought, Bourke was absently tapping his finger against his chin.

"Mark?"

He roused himself to say, "I know the McDonald case looks like a suicide-murder, not an accident, but there are some similarities to the ones Ren's talking about. For example, the beneficiary, Penelope Neale, made a big thing with the neighbor about what time she arrived at the crime scene."

"I've got a feeling about that one too, Mark. It'll be interesting to know if the policies on her sister and brother-in-law were recently increased."

"I'll get on it," said Bourke. "Maybe" — his grin was sardonic — "I'll ask Terry to follow it up. I do hope it'll be interesting enough for him."

Carol went in search of Superintendent Edgar, but he'd left for the day. She had no luck with her immediate superior, Chief Inspector Bertram, either, so she went back to her office and wrote a memo to Edgar, copy to Bertram, briefly detailing the points that Renwick Downing had raised.

It was, she cynically thought, an exercise in covering her back, even though she had very little but supposition to report. Jim Bertram wasn't a problem. He was rather ineffectual and it was somewhat of a mystery how he'd risen so far in the ranks, but Superintendent Edgar was something else again. Carol had learned the hard way the superintendent disliked surprises, and was ferocious if he believed he'd been put at a disadvantage because someone had failed to brief him thoroughly.

Although he demanded to be kept fully informed, Edgar was impatient with details, always wanting what he called 'the broad picture.' Carol had become quite adept in providing the super with more than he ever wanted to know. He found this reassuring, even though he generally skimmed through information, primarily to determine how it might affect him and his career.

In this instance she had very little in the way of concrete facts, but she detailed Ren Downing's concerns, and set out the names, dates and places, ending with a note that she would pursue the issue and report back when she had more data.

After leaving a voicemail message for Leota to say Aunt Sarah would be delighted to meet her on Saturday night, Carol packed her briefcase. On Thursday she'd requested a copy of the case notes on Barry Lyne's fatal fall. The information had arrived from the Blue Mountains that morning, but as yet she hadn't had time to read the report.

The offices around her were rapidly emptying and she joined the others anxious to start their weekends. When she reached her car she called Aunt Sarah on her mobile phone. "I'm just leaving work now. What do you want me to pick up for dinner? Pizza? Chinese? Whatever you fancy."

"Seeing as you need good, home-cooked food," said her aunt, "I've got a roast in the oven with all the trimmings, so hurry home, darling. I'll let you help me make the gravy, the way you used to when you were a kid."

Driving home, Carol considered how important Aunt Sarah had been to her for as long as she could remember. Images of childhood filled Carol's imagination. She could recall the joy of the long summer break from school, spending the lazy, hot summer days with Aunt Sarah and Uncle Paul in their weatherboard cottage in the Blue Mountains near the Gordon Falls, where water fell in lacy showers down the sheer sandstone cliffs to the sea of eucalyptus gums filling the flat floor of the valley below.

Carol, as a protected only child, had adored the freedom of playing with neighborhood kids, running wild along the bush trails, exploring the streams and waterfalls, unfettered by her parents' cautions and warnings. And late each afternoon coming home, hot and tired, to Aunt Sarah's cakes and buns, fresh out of the huge, black firewood stove in the comfortable, old-fashioned kitchen.

She could visualize Uncle Paul, skinny and laconic, smoking his pipe as he sat on the front veranda, birds calling in the fading light. Georgette, their patrician Siamese cat, would be sitting at his feet, idly surveying her domain. Sometimes Uncle Paul would tell tall tales in that serious, slow voice of his, conjuring up the legendary bunyips that were said to hide in the thickest bush near waterways, ready to leap out and seize unwary humans passing by. Carol could remember the delicious chill his stories caused her, a sense that unknown dangers lurked in the outside world, but here in her aunt and uncle's home she was safe and loved.

The Aunt Sarah of her childhood had shown the same inexhaustible energy, the exuberant love of nature and life, she still exhibited. Although Carol could see little physical change from the aunt of the past to the one of the present, she realized this must be a trick of memory. She knew that Aunt Sarah had once had blonde hair like Carol's, and that her face wouldn't have had the network of fine lines that webbed it now.

As she parked her car Carol anticipated the delicious scents of cooking that would be filling her house. She was not disappointed. Her mouth watered as she opened the front door. "Aunt Sarah! That smells wonderful."

"You look tired, darling. We'll relax with a drink, then eat early."

"Fine by me." She found herself smiling broadly. Coming home to this combination of someone who loved her and a delicious meal cooking was a delight that Carol had almost forgotten.

As she set the table — "Cloth napkins, Carol, not those paper things" — she thought again of the warm memories she had of the cottage in the mountains.

"I was thinking about Uncle Paul, and how he used to sit on your front veranda, smoking his pipe."

"There's no way I'd let him smoke if he were alive today," said Aunt Sarah severely. Her face softened. "I've told him so — after all these years I still find myself having conversations with him. And don't tell me I'm going mad, I've been doing it for years."

"I don't think you're mad," said Carol.

"Perhaps you'll change your mind when you hear that even now I often walk into the kitchen at home and feel surprised not to see him sitting there at the table, reading his paper."

Putting her arm around her aunt's shoulders to give her a squeeze, Carol said, "You were married a long time."

"Thirty-five years. Not long enough, my dear."

Without knowing quite why, Carol said, "When you first met Uncle Paul, did you know he was the one?"

"Heavens, no, darling! I thought he was a bit boring, if truth be told. He didn't say much and I hardly noticed him. Paul told me later that he'd got the impression I was rather a wild young thing, and not at all the sort of girl he was interested in."

"Were you wild?"

"Was I ever!" Aunt Sarah smiled reminiscently. "You have no idea . . . And don't ask for details. My lips are sealed."

"So if you thought he was boring, and he thought you were too wild, how did you and Uncle Paul ever get together?"

Cherished memories lighting her face, Aunt Sarah said, "There was a whole group of us, friends I'd had most of my life. We went to dances, movies, and generally had fun together. Paul was a friend of Kitty Lake's brother, and he sort of drifted into the group. I didn't pay much attention, but he was always around, and we got to know each other better. Then one day, out of the blue, I realized he was the only person in the world with whom I felt completely comfortable. I knew then that I would want to spend the rest of my life with him. Very fortunately, he felt the same way."

"So it wasn't a mad, impetuous love affair?"

"Of course it was. It was just that we began with a long, slow fuse." She gave Carol a keen look. "How important is this American to you?"

Caught off guard, Carol said, "What made you ask that?"

"Don't play for time, Carol. Just answer the question."

"Important. But how important I don't know yet."

"Hmmmm."

Alarmed by her aunt's thoughtful expression, Carol said, "You're not intending to give Leota the third degree, are you? I'm not going to let you two meet, if you are."

An innocent expression replaced the thoughtful one. "Why would you think I would do that?"

"Because I know you, aunt," said Carol with a reluctant smile.

"I'll be on my best behavior, I promise."

"Why is it," said Carol, "that I don't feel reassured?"

* * * * *

On Saturday morning Aunt Sarah dragged Carol out shopping, and they arrived home with the car packed with what Aunt Sarah categorized as "Good, healthy food."

"This really is a waste," Carol protested, as laden with grocery bags, she staggered down the path to the front door. "I won't eat half of this."

"You will, my dear, because I'll be here to make sure you do."

Realizing what she meant, Carol peered over the top of the bags she was holding to say, "There's a very good chance you'll be going back home to the mountains on Tuesday, so you'll have to take some of this with you."

"I don't think for one moment I'll be going home as soon as that." Aunt Sarah was brisk, matter-of-fact. "I'll almost certainly be having an operation, and I was rather hoping to stay here when I leave the hospital."

"Aunt Sarah . . ." began Carol, not knowing how to continue. Empty words of encouragement would be rightly scorned.

"Let's not talk about it, Carol. What happens, happens, and we'll know for sure Monday afternoon."

They spent the rest of the day quietly, Carol reading through the work she'd brought home, and Aunt Sarah puttering around the garden, secateurs in hand, snipping and pruning.

Late in the afternoon Aunt Sarah called her friend Lillian Broadhall, arranging for Carol to drive up to Leura the next morning to get background information on Barry Lyne and his family.

"Lillian's an invaluable member of Eco-Crones," she said, putting down the phone. "Straight to the point, and no nonsense. At a demo, if the police are called, we always place her in the front lines. Being a retired schoolteacher, Lillian's taught generations of kids in the district. Puts the cops at a bit of a disadvantage, you see, when she asks after their family members by name. I remember a sergeant at one demo was getting quite stroppy with us, when Lillian asked after his mum. Quite threw him off his stride."

"I don't know if I approve of intimidating the police," said Carol, laughing.

When Carol left at five-fifteen to collect Leota at her hotel in the city, Aunt Sarah walked her to the car. "I'm so looking forward to meeting Leota. You're not going to rush her in, then rush her straight out again, are you? I'd really like a chance to get to know her."

"That's what I'm afraid of," Carol muttered as she started the engine.

"What, dear?"

"Nothing. See you soon."

Carol glanced in the rear vision mirror before she turned the first corner, and saw her aunt, a short, plump, indomitable figure, standing in the carport looking after her.

Carol's heart quailed. What if her beloved Aunt Sarah should die?

"May I call you Aunt Sarah?"

Carol's aunt beamed at Leota Woolfe. "Of course you may." Her smile mischievous, she went on, "And I imagine I'm to call you Agent Leota. Yes?"

Leota's white teeth flashed in her dark face. "If you wish, but I'd prefer something less formal."

Carol stood back, gently amused at the contrast between the two. Leota, her black skin gleaming with health, her short hair groomed into a disciplined style, her sage green slacks and tunic top severely cut, seemed to tower over Aunt Sarah, who had changed for the occasion into a crimson smock and bright purple leggings. Carol noticed her aunt had clearly tried to do something with her hair, as a couple of cerise combs tried in vain to contain its exuberance.

"You know, Leota," said Aunt Sarah, head tilted in close examination, "I do believe bright colors would suit you very well."

"Thank you."

"I'm thinking a hot pink, or perhaps a deep chrome yellow? What do you think?"

Carol interposed. "Aunt Sarah..."

"Oh, yes, where are my manners? Do sit down, Leota, and make yourself comfortable. I know you're having dinner later, but I've made a few little appetizers to keep you going until then."

"I'll get them," said Carol.

When she came back with a tray of appetizers she found them chatting companionably. With foreboding Carol saw that her aunt was settling down for a spirited question and answer session. Her bright gaze fixed on Leota's face, she said, "Leota — it's a lovely name. Where does it come from?"

"I've no idea, I'm afraid."

"Tsk," said Aunt Sarah, "I find such lack of curiosity a little surprising in an FBI agent. I thought you investigated absolutely *everything*."

There was an emphasis on the last word that Carol didn't like. She'd frequently heard her aunt's opinion of the FBI, not to mention the CIA, ASIO, and similar government bodies, both local and international.

"Aunt Sarah," she said in her most quelling tone, "you're not intending to go all political, are you?"

"Of course not, Carol. Weren't you going to get us drinks, darling?"

Putting the tray on the coffee table between them, Carol said, "Frankly, I'm afraid to leave you two alone."

"Very wise," said Aunt Sarah, "as we'll be discussing you in depth the moment you leave the room."

"Then I'd better stay."

Aunt Sarah made a face at her. "A little sherry, please dear. Dry — I don't like the sweet stuff."

"Bourbon on the rocks?" said Leota, responding to Carol's interrogative look. "If you have it."

"Southern Comfort?"

"Great."

As Carol admitted defeat and went to get the drinks, she heard her aunt say, "So, Leota, tell me all about how you came to be here in Australia."

Later, in the car, Carol said, "Come clean. What did my aunt get out of you when I wasn't in the room?"

"Everything," said Leota, laughing. "I was helpless to resist. She makes FBI interrogation techniques look stone age."

CHAPTER NINE

Leota's suite had the comfortable anonymity that made hotel rooms so instantly forgettable. It was furnished in neutral shades and a generic artwork hung above the bed. Carol prowled around, thinking how neat Leota was. Everything was put away. Apart from a toothbrush and toilet articles in the bathroom, there was no evidence anyone was occupying the space.

"I've ordered champagne. French, of course," said Leota as Carol turned away from the window, where she'd been inspecting the impressive view of the city and harbor.

"What's your favorite color?"

"Yellow," Leota replied immediately. Then she thought about the question. "Well, goldish-yellow, to be more accurate." Grinning, she added, "It's my sunny personality, no doubt."

"No doubt."

Leota moved to take Carol in her arms. Her kiss, as always, ran fire down Carol's spine. "Wow," she said against Leota' lips, "instant ignition."

"So what's your favorite color?"

"Mine? I'm one of those conventional seven out of ten people. It's blue."

Sliding her hands down Carol's back, Leota murmured, "There's nothing the least conventional about you, my dear Inspector."

"Do you remember our first kiss? I recall it gave me quite a jolt."

"It was meant to."

They kissed again, slowly. Leota broke away first. "If we keep this up we'll never hear room service at the door, and that would be a pity. I want to toast you, and us, in champagne."

"A special occasion?"

"Honey, every occasion with you is special."

"Keep this sweet-talk going," said Carol, "and I'll be putty in your hands."

A sharp knock made them both laugh. The young man looked to Carol about her son's age, but he swept in, with a practiced flourish deposited the champagne flutes, red roses in a crystal vase and the silver stand containing the fat champagne bottle, whipped out the room account for Leota to sign, and was out the door, all within the space of a few seconds.

"Red roses for passion," said Leota, popping the champagne cork with an expert twist.

"To us." They solemnly saluted each other, then drank.

Carol had a weakness for champagne. She loved the fizz of bubbles in her mouth and the buzz it gave her. Alcohol was alcohol, no matter what form it took, but somehow champagne had a special quality, effervescing in her veins, filling her with a delightful lightness.

"Come to bed," Leota said, taking her hand.

"Why is it that when I'm with you it always seems like the first time?"

"My infinite variety?" said Leota, slipping off Carol's top.

"That must be it."

"You're shivering, Carol."

"Believe me, I'm not cold."

They stood naked, breast to breast, leaning into each other. At every point that Leota's dark skin touched Carol's a fire arose. Carol had thought she would be content to wait, savoring the sensory delight, but abruptly a relentless, glowing ache flamed into a compelling need for conquest, and for subjugation.

Seizing Leota, she kissed her deeply, her mouth demanding what her body was clamoring for with such burning urgency. They were on the bed, wrestling, questing, submerged in a battle to reach the height of all desire. To burst free, to fly, to forget the boundaries of body and mind.

Carol gloried in the taste, the scent of her, the sensuous slide of her skin, the strength in her arms, legs, back. The athletic demands she made on Carol's body.

"Ah, yes!" Carol was close, closer, over the top and exulting in the rhythms that sucked from her all consciousness of time, thought, fear.

Later, wet with sweat, lying within the curve of Leota's arm, reality came spinning back. Making love in hotel rooms, fitting each other in to busy schedules, never having the luxury of spending a lazy day together, reading, chatting, letting the time drift by.

Without meaning to, Carol put words to her thoughts. "I keep on wondering, is this the cake, or just the icing on the cake?"

"Icing? You mean frosting, I think. It's both, Carol."

This wasn't, Carol thought, a good enough answer. "To hell with cake philosophy," she said, turning until she pinned Leota beneath her. "You're like a drug," she whispered, gently biting Leota's earlobe. "I think I'm satisfied, but I never am. Not fully."

"You'll be sorry you said that," declared Leota, laughing. With one swift move she'd reversed their positions and held Carol prisoner. "You'll be begging for mercy, honey, before the night is over."

"Promises, promises." She gasped as Leota touched her. "Do your best," she said. "Please."

CHAPTER TEN

The next day Aunt Sarah had decided to accompany Carol to the Blue Mountains, saying she wanted to check on her house and make arrangements in case she was absent for a longer period than first expected. It was a clear, crisp day, the high winds sweeping the sky free of clouds, so that it glowed an incandescent blue. Although Carol had arrived home shortly before dawn, she insisted they leave early, and as the Sunday morning traffic was light, they made excellent time.

Carol smiled as they climbed into the mountains, feeling a shadow of the joyous anticipation she had always experienced when as a child her parents had driven up to visit Carol's aunt and uncle.

"Your house has hardly changed from when I was a kid,"

said Carol, drawing up outside the cottage. Like many old mountain homes of the same period it had wide verandas and walls of painted weatherboard. Carved posts at the edge of the front veranda supported the corrugated iron roof, which in Aunt Sarah's cottage was a deep red. Four wide stone steps led up to the front door, which, like the window trim, was a dark forest green that contrasted nicely with the deep cream color of the walls. The garden wasn't at its best this time of year, but its profusion still put Carol's efforts in Seaforth to shame.

Lillian Broadhall lived only a few streets away. Carol saw her aunt into the house, then walked to her appointment. It was cool, but Carol, hands shoved into the pockets of her windbreaker, strode along fully enjoying the wine of the unpolluted air and the balm of quietness.

There was an unhurried atmosphere, a feeling that time had slowed a little, and Carol felt her shoulders relaxing. She met several people on her walk, greeted them all, patted two dogs taking their owners for an outing — a cheerful golden retriever and a lugubrious basset hound — and arrived at her destination a few minutes early.

The house, although built in the same style as her aunt's, was much larger, painted dark green with lighter green door and window frames, and a sparkling silver roof. Unlike Aunt Sarah's, the veranda in the front had been enclosed with latticework, a mistake, Carol thought, as the sense of airy freedom an open veranda gave was lost.

The brass knocker was polished to a rich warm golden-brown. It was fashioned in the form of the head and shoulders of a lion, his jaws clamped around the heavy metal ring that Carol used to signal her arrival. She gave two quick knocks, and had hardly let her hand fall before the door was opened. The woman looked Carol up and down, gave a swift nod, and commanded, "Straight down the hall to the end, turn left."

Following these succinct instructions, Carol found herself in a charming room full of antique cane furniture lovingly restored to its full glory. The house had been built near the edge of the cliffs, and the view from the row of sliding windows was breathtaking. The drop to the valley floor was so great that treetops formed a gray-green carpet across which the shadows of clouds drifted.

"What a beautiful room," said Carol.

"Thank you. Take a seat."

Lillian Broadhall was tall and sinewy, with wavy, gray hair, a firm mouth and a direct gaze that Carol thought must surely have unsettled generations of school children.

Moving with the easy grace of one much younger than her years, Lillian crossed the room to where a large chrome cylinder squatted incongruously on a dainty cane table. "Coffee? Have it here in this thermos contraption. Prefer tea? I can make it."

"Coffee, black, please." Carol grinned to herself, thinking that the ex-teacher's terse manner of speaking seemed to be catching.

She handed Carol the coffee in delicate china that had a green and brown bamboo design curling up the side of the cup. "Sugar?"

She nodded approval when Carol shook her head. "Good. Epidemic of diabetes these days. Excessive sugar one cause."

After serving herself coffee in a china cup matching Carol's, she seated herself in an adjoining cane chair and said, "Do you run?" Enhanced by her precise diction, her voice, though not loud, had a carrying quality.

"I try to, every morning."

Lillian Broadhall bestowed another look of approval. "Excellent. Me? Running for years. Belong to a club. And still doing competitive events and getting good times. Beat the pants off other women my age." She shot Carol a challenging look. "You?"

"I don't run competitively."

"You should. It'll keep you young." She pursed her lips. "Mind, good genes help. Sarah's side of the family are good, strong stock. She's hardly had a day's sickness, to my knowledge. Likely to go on forever."

Forever? Please, yes, thought Carol. It was obvious Lillian had no idea that Aunt Sarah was facing the possibility of cancer.

"Need food with your coffee? Don't approve of eating between meals, but I can get you something."

"Thank you, no." Deciding to take the reins of this conversation before it got entirely away from her, Carol said, "Ms Broadhall, I've come to ask you some questions. I'm sure my aunt mentioned —"

"Lillian. Can't stand Lily or Lil." With the trace of a smile she added, "Got that?"

"Got it."

"Am I to call you Inspector?"

"Carol will be fine."

"Carol, then." She cocked her head to examine Carol closely. "Sarah's very proud of you. Now, what's this all about?"

"My aunt says that you're a font of knowledge about the Blue Mountains."

This praise elicited an affirmative grunt. "Should be. Lived here all my life, but can't claim to know everything."

"I'm interested in the family and friends of Barry Lyne."

Lillian's face darkened appreciably. Her voice sharp, she said, "A nasty man. Many said good riddance when he died."

"He wasn't popular?"

"He was very popular with a certain type. The sort that blather on about creating jobs and making the Blue Mountain economy vibrant." She gave a disgusted grunt. "Money-grubbers, out for what they can get. To hell with the little person and the environment. And they call it progress!"

"My aunt tells me the Eco-Crones demonstrated against the development Lyne was backing."

Abruptly, Lillian Broadhall smiled. She had large yellow teeth that looked strong enough to bite off someone's head.

"We put on an excellent show. Weren't the only ones. Part of a broad coalition of groups opposing the scheme."

"And this proposed development fell apart when Lyne died?"

"Thankfully, yes."

"Did you know Barry Lyne's wife?"

Emphatic nod. "I did. From childhood. Taught her when she was a little thing. Alyce Mure she was then. And a year after her was Alyce's brother, Ian. Inseparable."

"Aunt Sarah says Alyce left the area after her husband died."

"Wollongong."

"Wollongong?"

Lillian frowned. "Hard to believe, indeed. Alyce moved to Wollongong. Her brother, Ian, was there, so she joined him." Her face set in lines of extreme disapproval, she went on, "Industrial town, Wollongong. Can't imagine going from here to there, and being happy. Can you?"

"Ian's her only brother, I believe."

"No. Alyce had an older brother. Died when she was still at school."

"An accident?" said Carol, on high alert.

"You could say so. Fooling around on the platform of the local station. Fell under a fright train."

"Any doubt it *was* an accident?"

Lillian's thin lips had a cynical twist. "Fatty Mure, they called him. A bully. Never had the pleasure of teaching him, but knew about his exploits. He was running his own little protection racket. Terrorized the junior kids."

"So you're saying it wasn't an accident?"

"I'm saying not a tear was shed."

Carol asked some general questions about the Mure family. The parents had both died in a small plane crash while flying to snowfields in New Zealand's South Island. Alyce and Ian had been in their early twenties at the time. Lillian pointed out that from his teens Ian Mure had been in trouble with the

93

law, driving while intoxicated, arrests for fighting, and a couple of instances where he'd been caught trying to obtain proscribed drugs with forged paperwork.

As Lillian told it, a combination of personal charm, a penitent demeanor and efficient legal representation helped Ian avoid jail time. He'd apparently cleaned up his act after this close call, building a career for himself in local tourism, where he acted as liaison for all the disparate groups anxious to lure visitors to the area.

Just about the time his sister got married, he'd moved to Wollongong.

"If he was doing well here, why the move?" Carol asked.

"Not a clue. Whatever the reason, rest assured it'd be to Ian's advantage."

"How did Ian Mure get on with Barry Lyne?"

Lillian smiled thinly. "Looking for a reason for him to shove Lyne over Govetts Leap? Good luck. Ian and Barry Lyne were soulmates." She gave a bark of laughter. "If that term applies to their type."

"Soulmates how?"

"Rape the environment. Develop, develop, develop. That was their credo." She gestured at Carol's cup. "More coffee?"

"Thank you. It's excellent."

As Lillian filled Carol's cup, she declared, "Fresh coffee beans. Only way to go. You grind your own?"

"At times."

"Get into the habit. It's worth it."

Once they were both settled again, Carol said, "What's your personal opinion of Ian Mure?"

"A charmer. Indubitably. Good at talking his way out of difficulties. Could convince you black was white, green was red."

"I don't imagine he could convince you of anything much," said Carol, smiling.

"Didn't stop him trying. Ian was, and is, hard to dislike."

"And Alyce? What about her?"

Lillian pursed her lips. "She thinks the world owes her a living. Good-looking enough to have the world agree with her. Rules are for other people, not Alyce."

"What about her marriage?"

A snort. "Business proposition, both ways. Lyne got a beautiful wife other men envied. Alyce got money and social position."

"Were there problems?"

"Oh, yes." Lillian Broadhall grimaced. "Lyne was much older than Alyce. And jealous. A few weeks before he died she had emergency medical attention. Black eyes, bruises, a broken rib. That sort of thing."

Yesterday Carol had read through the case report on the investigation of Barry Lyne's death. There had been no mention of any trouble between husband and wife. "Was this common knowledge?" she asked.

"Alyce has pride. Saw her own doctor after hours. Kept it very quiet." She flashed her large-toothed smile at Carol. "And how do I know this? Doctor's wife's the daughter of a friend, Edie Bligh. Edie's an Eco-Crone, and a bit of a gossip, but only within our group."

"I'm wondering why the local police didn't mention the domestic violence."

"Can hazard a guess. Alyce was cozy with a cop. Owen Ingram. You should be asking him that question." She held up her forefinger in a warning gesture. "Be warned — Owen's quite the star in our local drama club. Not a bad actor, at all."

Armed with Sergeant Ingram's address, known by Lillian Broadhall because — "I sing with his sister in the church choir. I'm alto. You?" — Carol walked back to her aunt's place, told her she'd be an hour or so, and drove to the police officer's house in neighboring Katoomba.

"Owen Ingram?" She said to the man who opened the door

of the undistinguished brick house. When a teenager, he would have been handsome in a fleshy, high-colored way. Now he was a beefy, thick-necked man with a brick-red complexion who gave the impression of muscle slowly turning into fatty tissue.

"Who's asking?" he said in a truculent tone. His expression changed as he recognized her, "Inspector Ashton. What in the hell . . ."

"I have a few questions about Barry Lyne and his wife. You were the lead investigator on the case, I believe."

Ingram looked back over his shoulder. "Look, Inspector, the wife . . . she's expecting. Eight months gone. Could we talk in the yard? I don't want her disturbed."

They walked together down the side of the house and into the back yard, which was meticulously laid out with plots of vegetables. In one corner was a small glasshouse, its panes sparkling clean.

"Impressive," said Carol.

Ingram's tight expression mellowed for a moment. "I've got a bit of a green thumb. I like planting and growing things."

There was a wooden bench, bathed in sunlight, situated near the back fence. They sat down, one at each end, a meter of space between them. "What do you want to know?" he demanded, obviously feeling more comfortable away from the house. "The Lyne death was an accident."

"Some further questions have arisen. There's a possibility we may reopen the case as a homicide."

A fleeting expression of satisfaction crossed his heavy face. "Oh, yeah?" he said. "What sort of questions?"

It was hot in the sun. Carol let his query hang in the air as she stripped off her windjacket. She folded it and placed it between them. Then she said, "I want to know why the fact that Alyce Lyne was a victim of domestic violence was suppressed. It was germane to your inquiry, yet this fact doesn't

Ingram was silent, his face reflecting a struggle between two opposing desires. At a guess, Carol thought the need to cover his own back was competing with pleasure of having the case opened again.

"I get a feeling you want the Lyne case reopened," she said.

Taken aback, he blinked at her. "I didn't say that."

"Don't lie to protect yourself," said Carol crisply. "It's gone way beyond that. Just tell me the truth." Before he could respond, she went on, "It appears that one of the investigating officers had a close personal relationship with Alyce Lyne. I'm guessing the officer in question is you."

Involuntarily he looked toward the house. "Not me. You're barking up the wrong tree."

"Your name was mentioned."

He narrowed his eyes. "Who said that?"

"That's not material. What is important is whether or not it's true. I'm quite prepared to question every cop in the local station, if you prefer not to answer."

The possibility of his fellow officers being brought into it was clearly unwelcome. "Now, hold on —"

"It's very possible Barry Lyne was murdered. That makes the stakes a lot higher for you if you were involved."

His expression indecisive, he opened his mouth, then shut it again. A glance at Carol's stony face decided Ingram. "Okay." He dropped his voice to a near whisper. "We were just friends."

"Not the way I heard it."

"All right, a bit more than friends. But not after Allie married. It stopped right then." Flushed, he sent her a look of entreaty. "Look, does the wife have to know? I mean, it's over, and it'd only upset her . . ."

"Give me the whole story, Sergeant Ingram, and I'll see what damage control, if any, might apply."

He rubbed his forehead. "Jesus Christ, I was a fool to go along with it, but Allie begged me not to let anything get out about the way Lyne had bashed her. She told me she was ashamed, and her doctor would keep it quiet. Besides, she said, now Lyne was dead, what was the point of dirtying his good name?"

"That was enough to convince you to keep quiet?"

He moved uncomfortably. "Yeah . . ."

"And it never occurred to you this domestic violence gave Alyce Lyne a strong motive to kill her husband?"

"Allie wouldn't do that. I mean, I know her." He didn't sound totally convinced.

"I'll arrange to get a written statement from you, Ingram. Times, places, full details." Carol put up her hand as he started to protest. "If you cooperate, and are not materially involved in Lyne's death, I may be able to keep the information out of the media. That's all I can say."

"Materially involved?" For the first time Ingram realized the trouble he might be in. "I had nothing to do with it." He gave her a pleading look. "Honest, I just did a favor for a friend."

Recalling Lillian Broadhall's words about Ingram's theatrical ability, Carol wondered how much of what he'd said had been an act. "What did you expect in return?"

His red complexion deepened even further. "I don't know what you mean."

"Was there an understanding that you if you carried out this favor, Alyce Lyne would resume your former sexual relationship? Or had you done that already?"

"I —"

"The truth, please."

He spread his knees, clasping his hands between them. Bending his head so she couldn't see his eyes, he said in a low voice, "Allie told me that she was scared she'd be blamed for her husband's death, so she didn't want any mention of what he'd done to her to get out. She said . . ." His voice dropped to a whisper.

"I'm sorry, I can't hear you."

Ingram straightened, clearing his throat. "She said she'd always cared for me. Made it clear we'd pick up where we left off. Inspector, it's not like it sounds. I love my wife, but Allie —" He let out his breath in an explosive sigh. "Allie is something else."

Catching the impatience on Carol's face, he went on, "Allie said we'd have to wait until after the inquest. Then, without a word to me, she packed up and got out. Went to Wollongong. I tried calling her, but when I finally got hold of her, she pissed me off."

"She told you the affair was over?"

"In no uncertain terms."

"Have you spoken to her since then?"

"Not a word." His voice was bitter.

Carol thought that anything that made his ex-lover unhappy would be okay by Ingram.

"If Alyce Lyne contacts you I want you to play it cool, and not mention our conversation today. And call me immediately if she does. Do you understand?"

"Allie won't contact me." He added with scorn, "Why would she? There's nothing more I can do for her."

A point that had been niggling Carol since she'd read the police report on Lyne's death surfaced in her mind. "It was very early in the morning when Barry Lyne fell," she said.

"Yeah, around sunrise."

"He often ran that route on the trail that ran along the edge of the gorge."

"It's in the report. Now, if you don't mind . . ." He didn't bother to hide his impatience.

"And Alyce Lyne had arranged to meet her husband near the lookout and drive him home for breakfast."

"Yeah? So?"

"She had an alibi because she had a long conversation with a passerby. At that time of morning in that location I'm surprised that there was anyone else there at all."

Ingram raised his shoulders in a shrug. "The guy was fair

dinkum. Ken Stevens, his name was. A tourist from Bulli, out for an early morning stroll when he saw a good-looking woman drive up and park. Why wouldn't he stop and have a word or two?"

Wollongong, where Alyce Lyne's brother Ian had moved after his sister's wedding, was on the coast about sixty kilometers south of Sydney. Bulli, a little settlement, was situated a few kilometers north of Wollongong. Coincidences do happen, Carol thought, but this one was worth checking out.

Ingram had got to his feet, an unsubtle message that he wanted Carol out of there. She obligingly stood, put on her windjacket, and said, "Where were you that morning, Sergeant Ingram, when Lyne died?"

"Me?" His anger and astonishment were plain. "You're bloody asking *me* for an alibi?"

When Carol didn't respond, he snapped, "Jesus Christ! I was in bed with my wife. Okay? And she'll vouch for that, so you can forget accusing me of anything."

"It's not the best of alibis," Carol observed.

"It happens to be the truth. I was still in bed when they called me to say someone had been killed at Govetts Leap. You can check, if you like."

Ingram saw Carol off his property with unflattering haste, and disappeared inside the house even before she had reached her car. She drove back to her aunt's place puzzling over Ingram's role. Perhaps he had just done a favor for a former lover, whose husband really had died in an accidental fall. Or perhaps he was up to his eyebrows in the cover-up of a murder. Or, more intriguingly, perhaps Ingram had killed Lyne himself. If so, he'd really been double-crossed when Alyce moved away.

She found Aunt Sarah in the kitchen, taking a tray of hot scones from the over. "I thought you'd need something before we set off for Sydney," she said.

Suddenly overcome with hunger, Carol was tempted to snatch one of the hot, steaming scones and cram it in her mouth. "Butter? Jam? Cream?" she said.

"The works," said Aunt Sarah, complacent.

CHAPTER ELEVEN

Carol went into work early on Monday morning to get through as much work as possible before she left to pick up Aunt Sarah for her afternoon appointment at the clinic. As usual Bourke was also there early. She took the opportunity to bring him up to date on her conversations with Lillian Broadhall and Ingram, and asked him to arrange for a statement to be taken from Ingram.

"Are you leaning towards him as the one who pushed Lyne into the gorge?" asked Bourke, adding, "As the investigating officer, he was in a terrific position to make sure the inquest found it was accidental death."

"I'm still not sure it wasn't simply an accident, but if not, perhaps the brother was involved. According to Lillian

Broadhall, Ian Mure was extremely close to his sister. Or maybe Alyce did the deed herself."

"From all I've heard, she doesn't strike me as the type," said Bourke. "I see her as a sort of femme fatale, pulling the strings while we poor males do all the work."

"Fancy a road trip?" said Carol. "I think it's worth while seeing Ken Stevens, the guy from Bulli that provided the alibi. And while we're in the area, Mark, we might as well go on to Wollongong and check out Ian Mure."

"Paulette Bruehl's husband lives in Wollongong." He raised his eyebrows. "The coincidences keep on coming, don't they?"

Later in the morning Liz Carey called in to see Carol. She plopped her boxy body into a chair and said, "How's tricks?"

"Busy as hell. They just keep dying."

Liz grinned at Carol's levity. "Tell me about it," she said with feeling. "I'm so behind on paperwork I thought I'd better pop in and give you a few preliminary details in person."

Carol sat forward, her eyes on the folder Liz was holding. "Anything interesting?"

"Not in the Trelawney case. I've already told you the fingerprints were no go. From the start it was an impossible crime scene. The area where the body landed was covered by salt water before we arrived, and there was bugger-all to find at the top of the cliff."

"So you're here about the McDonald shootings."

"Spot on. Are you still going for the scenario where McDonald kills his wife, then blows his own head off?"

"Unless you've got evidence to the contrary."

"Not exactly, although we've got a lot still to process. One thing really hit me and I thought you should know."

"Mark's with me on this one. Shall I call him in?"

"I've always got time for the sexy Sergeant Bourke," said

Liz with a wolfish grin, ruffling her gray hair, "but he never seems to have time for me."

Bourke entered with a mug of coffee in one hand. "Hey, Liz," he said, "can I get you a coffee?"

Liz rolled her eyes. "Poison me, would you?"

"I'll take that as a no." He settled himself in the chair across from Liz. "What's up?"

"Liz is about to reveal something interesting about the McDonald case," said Carol.

"I am." Liz handed each a photocopy from her folder. "I believe you were present when Urban found this."

The photocopy was of the piece of blood-stained paper that had been on the floor of the McDonald kitchen. Carol read it again: *Darling, darling Faye, please don't tell him anything about us just say you're leav . . .*

"We thought at the time it looked like part of a print-out of an e-mail," Carol said. "You can just see the beginning of the subject line."

"It does seem to be an e-mail," said Liz. "Standard ink-jet printer, totally untraceable, of course. Ah, for the days of type-writers."

She jabbed a square-nailed forefinger at the photocopy Carol held. "There's two things I find interesting. First, look at the way the paper's been torn, so that you get the word 'Subj:' to indicate it is an e-mail, but the heading itself, the date and details of sender are conveniently missing. Half of Faye McDonald's e-mail address is under that bloodstain you can see. Then note how the torn edge passes through the word 'leaving,' removing half of that line and the rest of the page, including the area where you'd expect the sender to put his name."

Bourke peered at his copy. "So you're saying this has been torn with a purpose?"

"It sure looks that way to me. Think about how you'd normally tear up a sheet of paper." Liz mimed ripping a page in half, putting the two pieces together and ripping it in half again. "You want to get rid of it, you either screw the page into a ball, or you rip it up into roughly square bits. And if it's really incriminating, you shred it — and the McDonalds had a shredder in their home office. Looks very suspicious to me." She added with sly smile, "But hell, you're the detectives."

"Thanks, Liz, for the vote of confidence," said Carol. "I believe you mentioned two things . . .?"

"It's what *wasn't* at the scene. No sign anywhere in the house of the rest of this page. Let's say McDonald confronts his wife with the e-mail, accusing her of having a lover on the side. Where does he get the e-mail from? And why tear it up? Is she carrying her a fragment of her lover's message around with her? If she's keeping it, why would *she* tear it?"

Liz made a face. "Another thing worries me. We'd taken the shotgun from the crime scene before you got there, Carol, so you didn't see it. It's a substantial weapon, a full-size double-barreled gun, and I'd say McDonald would have a hell of job holding it and shooting himself the way he's supposed to have. When I get a moment I'll go down to the morgue to have another look at the bodies before Duke carves them up. Take some more measurements and see if it's feasible he killed himself that way."

"There's powder residue on McDonald's hands?"

"There is, Mark, although I want to take another look at that, too."

After Liz had gone, Carol and Bourke sat and discussed the points she had raised. "It's hardly enough to justify a double murder investigation," said Carol, "but it certainly warrants more attention. Who can you put on it?"

"Terry can do it. He's already checking out the McDonalds' life insurance."

Carol checked the time. "Mark, I'll be out most of the afternoon. Call me on my mobile as soon as the Trelawney post mortem is finished. Oh, and while you're there, tell Jeff Duke we need the posts on Joseph and Faye McDonald as quickly as possible."

"Jeff falls for your charm rather more than mine," Bourke observed.

Carol knew he wasn't saying this to point out that she should be the one attending the Trelawney post mortem, not him, but she felt vaguely guilty anyway. If she could tell Bourke about Aunt Sarah he'd understand why Carol had asked him to step in, but her aunt clearly didn't want anyone else to know.

"I'll try and catch him on the phone," she said, without much hope that she could. The pathologist was notoriously difficult to find in his office.

Just before she left to collect Aunt Sarah she tried Jeff Duke's number and was surprised to have his booming voice answer. "Carol, how many times have you asked me to juggle the schedule?"

"Lots, Jeff, but you know I wouldn't ask if it wasn't important."

"You always say that. Sorry, Carol, but this time I can't help you. I've got corpses stacked to the ceiling. Friday's the best I can do."

"Friday? Jeff, this is urgent."

He grumbled to himself. "All right, Thursday morning, eleven o'clock. You'll be attending?"

"Yes."

"Terrific. See you then."

She fretted at the delay, and would have argued for a time on Wednesday, but Duke had a soft spot for Carol. She knew he would have moved the McDonalds further up in the schedule if he'd been able to do so.

Realizing she was running late, Carol sped home to find Aunt Sarah anxiously pacing the front path. They made record time to the clinic, arriving exactly at the appointed time.

Dr. Wu was ten minutes late, and full of apologies. Aunt Sarah, looking drawn, said, "Is it cancer?"

"I'm afraid so. The lump you have in your breast is cancerous, but the tumor isn't large, which means we seem to have caught it early. This is good news, because it almost certainly means the malignancy is confined to a small area."

As she took her aunt's hand, Carol felt numb. It was the news she'd been expecting. The hope had always been there that the lump was some anomaly, looking dangerous, but turning out to be harmless. Now that optimistic thought was gone. The reality was all too harsh.

Dr. Wu had leapt to her feet and was busily drawing diagrams on a whiteboard, explaining as she did so where the tumor was located and what the surgery options were. "During the operation your surgeon, Dr. Ristow, will be removing lymph nodes under your arm, here, to make sure the cancer hasn't spread."

Carol squeezed Aunt Sarah's hand. Her aunt didn't appear to notice, saying to Dr. Wu, "And if it has spread?"

"Then we need to be more aggressive in our treatment. However in your case, I'm very hopeful that it's only affected a limited area."

Carol struggled to concentrate on what the doctor was saying. Dr. Wu had said she was hopeful. Were these just standard, soothing words, or did she mean what she said?

Aunt Sarah, sitting stiffly to attention, asked, "Who decides? Will it be the whole breast? I mean, will the surgeon . . ."

"As you know, you have two options: mastectomy, where the whole breast and nearby lymph glands are removed, or lumpectomy, which entails removal of the tumor and surrounding tissue, plus lymph nodes, but essentially leaves you with your breast largely intact. Dr. Ristow will be discussing the pros and cons of both options with you."

"You haven't answered my question," said Aunt Sarah with a hint of her usual fire.

Dr. Wu grinned. "You decide," she said. Your surgeon discusses the whole issue with you, and he will also arrange for you to meet your oncologist, Dr. Yeats, who will be involved in post-operative treatment. In your case it's likely to be radiation therapy, which will target any stray malignant cells that may still be in the area."

"Not chemotherapy?" said Carol.

"That doesn't seem indicated."

Aunt Sarah looked a little brighter at this. Carol didn't blame her. Chemo, as she knew from the experiences of a friend who'd had the procedure, could be arduous.

Dr. Wu was pleased to go through the information again, answering questions in, Carol noted, the most positive way. Before they left her office, she called the surgeon and arranged an appointment for the next morning. Knowing she couldn't really spare the time, Carol said she would be there too.

As she ushered them out, Dr. Wu said, "One last thought to take away with you. Cancer can be beaten. It's not a death sentence."

Carol and her aunt went to the car in silence, the enormity of the diagnosis sinking in. Carol was almost relieved when her phone rang. It was Bourke.

"I'm back from Trelawney's post," he said. "Jeff says someone hit him, hard, on the back of the head, before he went over the cliff. It was something like a cosh, or a length of pipe, leaving a distinct indentation. It was pure luck the body landed as it did, face down, or the evidence would have been destroyed."

"I'll be in the office as soon as I can. If it's possible, line up an interview with Trelawney's widow for late this afternoon. Tell her we'll come to her place."

She disconnected, said to her aunt, "I promised to call Sybil," and dialed her work number.

At first there was silence at the news. Then Sybil, a tremor in her voice, said, "God, I've been expecting this, like we all have, but now it's definite . . . How's Aunt Sarah? Is she there with you?"

"We're outside the clinic. Sybil, I have to go back to work, and —"

"I'll meet you at the house. I'll stay with her until you get home."

Frowning, Aunt Sarah snapped, "What are you arranging? I don't need babysitting."

Carol repeated her comment to Sybil, who said, "Put her on."

It was a short conversation. Aunt Sarah handed the mobile phone back to Carol, saying ungraciously, "It isn't at all necessary, you know, but Sybil's insisting on coming over."

"Neither of us want you to be alone this afternoon. You know the old saying, a trouble shared is a trouble halved."

The anger that seemed to be buoying her up suddenly leaked away. She nodded slowly. "Thank you, darling."

Somehow this acquiescence upset Carol more than if her aunt had continued to demonstrate uncharacteristic hostility.

Terry Roham met Carol in the corridor outside her office. "You know the McDonalds? The policies were increased just two months ago."

With an effort, Carol forced her attention from her aunt to Roham's words. "Say that again."

"Australasian Fire and Life holds policies on the three business partners, Joseph and Faye McDonald, and Penelope Neale. Two months ago the policies were increased to a million apiece, the money going to the surviving partner or partners." He was almost dancing with enthusiasm. "Interesting, isn't it?"

"Very," said Carol. "Has Mark told you to concentrate on this case?"

"He has!" Roham beamed at her. "I think Liz Carey's right

about the torn paper, so it probably is a double murder." This possibility was plainly a source of great pleasure.

"How would you accomplish it, Terry, if you set out to get rid of two people this way?"

"Me?" He paused, then said, "If it's the sister, she has to have someone to do the dirty work while she makes sure she's free and clear. That's obvious."

"But that's just one possible suspect. What you need to find out is if there are others. Did either of the McDonalds have enemies? Is Penelope Neale the only person who benefits from their deaths? And if it is her, who would she trust enough to deputize to carry out the hit?"

With trepidation, she saw that Roham's face was flushed with almost religious zeal. "Terry," she said firmly, "always remember that you are under Mark Bourke's supervision. You are not to interview any witnesses by yourself. Check everything out with Mark before you do it, and don't under any circumstances go off on your own. If you can't find Mark, speak to me."

"Trust me," he said, "I won't make a move without making sure it's okay."

She watched Roham lope off down the corridor, enthusiasm almost sparking the air around him. She wished she could feel more confidence that he'd follow her instructions.

There was little time to consider if Terry Roham would be a hindrance, rather than a help, as she was almost immediately summoned to Superintendent Edgar's office. Chief Inspector Bertram was also present, wearing his customary faintly puzzled expression.

"What in the hell is all this?" demanded Edgar, flapping Carol's memo. "Just what's going on, Carol?"

She spent half an hour outlining the developing possibility that Ren Downing's theory was correct, and there was a murder-for-hire killer operating in New South Wales. She ended by pointing out that John Trelawney was a classic example of a death that had seemed so obviously an accident, but was now presenting as a murder because of the post mortem findings.

Edgar was predictably incensed, acting as though it were Carol's responsibility that this regrettable situation had occurred. Then, apparently realizing the media attention this could generate — Carol cynically imagined him visualizing the headline EDGAR'S COUP: FOR HIRE KILLER ARREST — he promised all the resources she would need, appointed Bertram to act as liaison with all other police jurisdictions that might be involved, and ordered both of them to keep him fully informed.

"And I mean *fully* informed. I'll be speaking with the Commissioner to alert him to the situation. Carol, I want a detailed report on my desk as soon as possible. Jim, from you I want a list of those in charge of each jurisdiction. I'll be contacting each of them personally."

"It's hit the fan with a vengeance," said Carol as she met Bourke outside Evelyn Trelawney's substantial brick house. She and Bourke had driven there separately, as Carol's home was only ten minutes away, and she was anxious to get back to see Aunt Sarah.

"So what's the superintendent's take on the situation?"

Carol smiled without humor. "What you'd expect. Ideally he'd prefer the whole multiple murder-for-hire idea to fade away, but if that doesn't happen, he'd like us to arrest the perp as quickly as possible so he can take the credit."

"My, my," said Bourke, "you are getting cynical in your old age."

Evelyn Trelawney's high, piping voice intruded from the front door. "Inspector, do come in. I've been watching out for you. And you're Sergeant Bourke. You've got such a nice voice on the phone."

She ushered them inside. "I've made tea. I hope you'll

have some of my fruit cake. In my own little circle I'm quite famous for it."

This was not the same woman that Carol had met in the parking area on North Head. Now her straight gray hair seemed to have more bounce, her body language was more definite, the tone of her voice more decided. Widowhood, Carol thought, became Evelyn Trelawney.

The furnishings of the house were utilitarian, the color scheme determinedly neutral. Evelyn took them into a sitting room at the rear that was quite different to the rest, as it was crowded with two pink upholstered sofas and matching chairs upon which many pink, frilly cushions were arranged.

"The Captain let me have this room as my own," she said. "He never set foot in it. Said it made him feel uncomfortable. Maintained it was too flowery and feminine for him."

She fussed over them until they were seated in matching pink chairs, then poured the tea and handed them pink cups. "My favorite color," she said. "I've read they use pink to soothe the insane, and I can see why it would work."

Carol signaled to Bourke that he should start the interview. He said, "This is excellent tea."

"Thank you. It's the type I like — the Captain preferred a harsher blend of black tea. He had it imported from Ceylon."

"We're here about your husband," said Bourke. "Had he any enemies?"

Evelyn sucked in her lips like a little girl. "He could be very abrupt. Offended people without meaning to do so . . ." She sent Carol a conspiratorial look. "You understand, don't you, Inspector? Men can say and do things without having the slightest idea of how their actions are being perceived. I'm sure you agree."

"We're not thinking of people your husband might have offended," said Bourke. "Was there anyone who would actively wish him harm?"

"His daughter, Dianne." Evelyn spat out the name with

112

venom. "She fought with the Captain almost every time they met."

Carol said, "You mentioned before that you believed his daughter could have pushed him over the cliff."

"I didn't really mean it. I was angry with her."

"Ms. Beaton mentioned that she believed your husband was showing signs of Alzheimer's disease," said Carol.

"John was a bit forgetful, like anyone his age . . ." Her voice trailed off.

"When I spoke with you at North Head," said Carol, leaning forward in a confidential manner, "you were very upset."

"Yes, yes, I was."

"I'm presuming that's why you forgot to inform me that you and your husband had a violent argument in the parking area before he went to watch the shipping."

Evelyn Trelawney was clearly stricken. Tea slopped into the saucer as she put down her cup with a shaking hand. "Someone else was there?" she breathed.

"The fight between you was witnessed by a man birdwatching. He described your husband as abusive and that you were crying."

Evelyn put her hands over her face. "This is terrible. I can't . . ."

Carol and Bourke remained silent. Evelyn put her hands down and looked from one to the other. "I am so embarrassed," she said. "To be truthful, Inspector, the Captain was becoming very difficult. I worried about his driving, but he snapped my head off every time I tried to say something. And he became so short-tempered. The smallest thing would set him off. He'd always been so proud of his forbearance, his command over his emotions, so when he began to . . . I knew if he realized how he was behaving he'd be horrified, ashamed."

Carol said gently, "Did you seek medical treatment?"

"When the Captain had his yearly check-up, our doctor took me aside and said that John had some cognitive impairment. I asked if it were Alzheimer's disease, and he said he thought so, although there were further tests that could be done. I tried to talk the Captain into having treatment, but he refused to admit that anything was wrong."

"It's hard, when someone's headstrong," Carol said sympathetically.

"I knew you'd understand, Inspector." A sudden concern crossed her face. "Why were you asking about enemies? Did John do something that I don't know about? He was very secretive at times."

Bourke said, "There's some evidence that your husband's death may not have been an accident."

Evelyn Trelawney's hands fluttered on her lap. "Not an accident? You mean he killed himself?"

Deliberately blunt, Carol said, "Not suicide. Murder. Someone struck a blow to his head."

Evelyn Trelawney stared at her. "I don't understand."

"Your husband was hit on the head before he fell."

"Murder? And all this time I thought it could have been my fault. That I'd upset John so much that he went to the top of the cliff in a rage, and didn't notice how close he was to the edge."

She got to her feet in a rush, her teacup falling to smash on the floor. She didn't seem to notice. "Who did this? Dianne? There's no one else who hated the Captain. No one."

Outside, Bourke said to Carol, "You know, she may be right."

"Evelyn Trelawney's got as much evidence of that as we have," said Carol sourly. "That is, zilch."

CHAPTER TWELVE

"I'm getting a taxi," said Aunt Sarah in the firm tone she used when she would brook no contradiction. "I know you have a load of work to do, so after we see the doctor, you go on to the city, and I'll catch a taxi home."

They were waiting in yet another medical room. Carol felt her skin prickle with antipathy. She had always disliked going to doctors, visiting hospitals, or dealing with medical staff in general. It was probably a matter of control, because she was quite aware she didn't feel this way when operating in her professional capacity, where she had some clout, and wasn't playing a supplicant role.

When Dr. Ristow hurried in, running late, he turned out to be a little man with a Hitler mustache and short wiry red hair. "I'm the stereotypical doctor," he announced. "Never on time. Sorry."

Carol's initial unfavorable impression disappeared as his essential kindness and consideration began to show. He examined Aunt Sarah's file closely, answered her questions comprehensively, and reassured them both that Aunt Sarah's decision to have a lumpectomy was exactly the one he would make in her place. He did point out that as he would be removing the lymph nodes under her right arm, and she was right-handed, that there would be some discomfort and restriction of movement. "I wouldn't go out and paint the house all day," he commented.

The operation was scheduled for early Thursday morning. "You'll be my first, when I'm fresh," he said with a smile.

When Dr. Ristow was sure they had no more questions or concerns, he called in Dr. Yeats, the oncologist who'd be monitoring the post-operative treatment.

He too, was supportive, reassuring Aunt Sarah that radiation treatment would not cause her to lose her hair, but might result in some fatigue. "Frankly," he said, "it's not the radiation that's tiring, it's the fact that you have it five days a week for seven weeks, so you get very bored with the whole thing. Mind you, it's only fifteen minutes a visit, and you'll have your own time slot, so you'll be in and out like a shot."

By the time they left the two doctors Aunt Sarah had become considerably more animated. "Really, darling," she said as they waited for the cab Carol had called, "they make it seem a lot less daunting than I'd thought. I mean, it's a pest and a bore, but I'm beginning to feel quite optimistic. I just have to get through the operation on Thursday, follow up with the radiation, and then I can forget about breast cancer and get my life going again."

Carol smilingly agreed, although she was sure that there were difficult times ahead. Her aunt was precisely the type of person who would go out and paint the house all day, and to hell with the consequences.

Bourke sat on the other side of Carol's desk with a laptop perched on his knees. "Poised for incoming notes," he declared. "But don't talk too fast."

"When's Dianne Beaton coming in?"

"We've got an hour, so let's get started."

Carol said, "Assuming we do have someone operating as a hitman, or woman, let's call the person X. So, Mark, how does X find clients? It's not a service you can advertise in the classifieds, or put in the yellow pages."

"Word of mouth?" He grinned. "I like the idea of testimonials from satisfied customers."

"How about through the Internet, in a chatroom, say, where people can bitch about their lives and people they hate?"

Bourke's fingers tapped the keys. He frowned at the screen, made a correction, then said, "I'm thinking there might be some sort of connection to the insurance companies. How about an employee who's assessing possible clients and passing the information on to X?"

"That's possible, although that would be a security risk for X. The more people involved, the more dangerous it becomes. Okay, the next question is how X approaches the potential client. How would you go about that?"

"Very carefully," said Bourke with a laugh. "You don't want the person you approach blowing the whistle on you."

"If it were me," said Carol, "I'd make sure that no one could identify me, at least until I was absolutely sure the would-be client was fully committed to the murder, and even then there'd be a chance it was a set-up. That means I'd use the phone, or possibly e-mail, as long as I could mask my return address."

"That's not hard to do," said Bourke, who'd recently done a course on e-mail fraud, "but it has the problem of leaving a written record."

Carol sat up. "Mark, put a note that we might consider confiscating suspects' computers, both at their workplace, and at home."

"So done," said Bourke, rattling the keys of the laptop.

"Your typing's improving," Carol observed.

Bourke frowned at her. "Please! Keyboard skills is the term. If you call it typing, we males won't be interested."

Carol tapped her forefinger against her lips. "When X has a hot prospect, the idea would be to get some cash, fast. If someone's willing to outlay a substantial sum, then X could assume the client was serious."

"What would you think a fair charge for murder?" Bourke asked. "Ten thou? Twenty? A set fee, our would you base it on a sliding scale, according to difficulty?"

"Maybe it would be based on ability to pay. It makes sense to have two installments, so there's a good faith deposit before the murder, and then the rest is due after the hit is success-fully carried out. Put in a note to look out for unusual bank withdrawals."

Carol smiled as Bourke, tongue in the corner of his mouth, concentrated on putting this point into the laptop. "What do you think," she said, "will that little computer take over from your written notes?" Bourke's notebooks, filled with his neat handwriting, were exemplary records.

"No way. I reckon witnesses will clam up if I whip out a laptop and start inputting whatever they say."

Carol got up to stretch. She walked around to look over his shoulder at the screen. "So now X has got the payment schedule in place, I imagine the next step is to research the victim's movements and pick a suitable time and place for the kill."

"And method," said Bourke. "Of the seven cases we're looking at, five are falls, one apparent suicide by car exhaust, and one a hit-and-run. As long as you can lure your victim to a suitable place, a fatal fall strikes me as the least hassle."

"At this point," said Carol, going back behind her desk, "X has the payment schedule set up, the method established, and has advised the client of exactly the time period the alibi needs to cover."

"If I were X," said Bourke, "I think this would be the time to give tutorial, a guide to what to do and say when the cops arrive. You don't want your client breaking down and admitting he or she has hired a hitman."

"Speaking of advice, we've forgotten the insurance angle," said Carol. "There's no point in setting up a murder before the victim's life is worth it."

"You think a percentage of the payout is the final sum?"

"Makes sense to me," said Carol, "But what if the client reneges, and doesn't come up with the post-murder payment because the deed is done and X can hardly run to the authorities and complain?"

"Rather dangerous to cross a professional murderer," said Bourke with a grin. "You'd spend the rest of your life glancing back over your shoulder."

"We could look for that," said Carol. "A victim fitting the pattern, followed some time after by the death of the beneficiary."

Bourke wasn't convinced. "I'll add it to the list, Carol, but I'd say X would cut his losses if a doublecross like that occurred, and not run the risk of being caught while carrying out an unnecessary murder."

He worked away for a few moments, then swung the laptop around so Carol could see the screen. It read:

Identify potential client (Internet? insurance company?)
Approach client (phone? e-mail?)
N.B. confiscate suspects' computers

Establish payment schedule (pre and post-murder?)
N.B. check for unusual bank withdrawals
Advise client to increase victim's life insurance
Research victim's movements
Establish kill method
Set firm time for hit to allow alibi
Get pre-murder payment
Carry out the hit
Get final post-murder payment
If client refuses payment, eliminate him/her?

"I've been thinking," Carol said, "that there's something else we should look for. It's probable there was some defining moment when X said 'I can do that.' I'm guessing he accomplished a murder of his own and got away with it easily, then decided to set up shop. Or perhaps he was involved in some way in a genuine accident, and saw the potential for rigging a murder to look accidental."

"The first one of the suspicious deaths we're looking at is Paulette Bruehl, and there was only a small policy on her life, so maybe that fits your theory."

Carol looked at the typed list of cases on her desk. "In chronological order, Paulette Breuhl is followed by Ursula Stein, who dies in a garage with a car running, then it's Barry Lyne at Govetts Leap, Wayne Cronnite gets hit by a car, Cindy Dunn falls down stairs, Hilda Perry drowns after falling off a small headland, and finally last week John Trelawney at North Head. All of these occur within a period of eighteen months."

"Ursula Stein seems an odd one out," said Bourke. "Much harder to set up, for one thing."

"Yes, but her husband fits the profile. She has the money in the family, her life insurance was increased a month or so before she died, and her husband goes to much trouble, according to the investigating officer, to make sure that everyone knows he has an alibi. In fact, he causes a scene in a restaurant, the police are called, and he's in custody when his wife dies."

"When post mortems on Joseph and Faye are completed on Thursday," said Bourke, "I've got the sinking feeling we'll be adding them to our list of X's accomplishments."

Carol's phone gave a preemptory ring. Dianne Beaton was waiting downstairs. Bourke went to collect her while Carol quickly skimmed over the alibi she'd given.

The woman shown into her office had a distinct resemblance to her father, having the same upright stance, arrogant nose and decisive jawline that Carol had seen in the photographs. Her eyes, as Bourke had said, were hard, as was her thin-lipped mouth. She was well-groomed, and wearing what was clearly a very expensive ruby suit.

"I'm co-operating by coming here," she said, ignoring Carol's outstretched hand. Sitting down in the chair Bourke had recently vacated, she cast a cold glance around the room.

"Not very impressive for Detective Inspector Carol Ashton," she said with disdain. "I would have expected something much more upmarket." She had a harsh, discordant voice that suited very well her tone of spiteful malice.

Quite a charmer, thought Carol. Aloud she said mildly, "We don't do our own interior decoration."

"Obviously not." She jerked her chin to indicate Bourke, who had taken the other chair. "Your sergeant here has already interviewed me. I figured if you wanted to see me, Inspector, there must be something up. What is it? Has Evelyn gone bonkers again and accused me of offing my father? If so, I must remind you that I couldn't possibly have had anything to do with him falling off North Head."

"I'm afraid I must tell you, Ms. Beaton, that the post mortem indicates that your father was almost certainly murdered."

For a moment Dianne Beaton's face went slack, then the

121

flinty mask was on again. "Oh, yes? I'd say the old man would be pretty well smashed up after a fall like that, so how could you find that out?"

"There was sufficient evidence."

"Of what, exactly?"

Carol said, "He was deliberately struck on the head."

"You can tell that? I don't believe it."

Bourke remarked, "I was there for the post mortem. The pathologist is very sure."

There was silence for a moment, then Dianne Beaton shook her shoulders as though shrugging off a weight. "Murder, suicide, accident, it makes no difference to me. My father is just as dead."

"It seems he had the signs of early Alzheimer's," said Carol.

"You say early, do you? Well-advanced, in my opinion."

"Why do you say that?"

For the first time, Dianne Beaton looked upset. "I couldn't believe how he'd changed from the father I'd known all my life. He used always had time for me, but lately . . ." There was a sheen of tears in her eyes.

"Lately?" Carol prompted.

"There were times my father didn't recognize me. He'd look at me like I was a stranger." She blinked rapidly, then went on, her voice hardening, "He often didn't know where he was. And foul-mouthed rages —" She shook her head.

"He was threatening to cut you out of his will."

Dianne Beaton shrugged. "He threatened that all the time. He never did it."

"So you inherit."

"Yes, I inherit. Of course a goodly portion goes to Evelyn." An unexpected smile curved her thin mouth. "And God knows, she deserves every cent. I don't have much time for Evelyn, but she never complained, and living with the Captain the way he was would try the patience of a saint."

Carol allowed another silence to grow. Finally, Dianne

Beaton said, "Evelyn was there at North Head. How come you're not accusing her? She's a bit fluttery, I know, but she's got a will like iron when she sets her mind to it. She could have followed him and bopped him with something, couldn't she?"

After she'd swept out, Bourke said to Carol, "Please let it be her."

"It could be either of them, Mark."

"Not Evelyn Trelawney, that sweet little old lady?" said Bourke in joking denial.

"True, her type usually poisons," said Carol, "but if you contract out the job, what does it matter how it's done, as long as it is?"

CHAPTER THIRTEEN

The noise in the briefing room dropped appreciably when Carol entered with Mark Bourke behind her. He distributed folders to everyone as Carol took her position at the front of the room. She surveyed the people in front of her. Everyone there was working close to capacity, even without the added burden of re-examining these now-suspicious cases. When Carol had asked for more resources, she'd been given platitudes about doing the best she could with what she'd got. When she pressed the issue, Maureen Oatland, a tough, experienced officer with whom Carol had worked before, was temporarily transferred to assist her.

On the whole she had a good team. Anne Newsome shone. Boyish Miles Li, frequently mocked for his youthful appearance, was showing signs of developing into an excellent investigator. Dennis Earl and Nanette Gates, the newest additions, seemed sound. Then there was Terry Roham, who might, with careful handling, become a competent officer. At the moment Terry was directly in front of her, talking to Maureen Oatland, whose substantial body and loud voice caused her to stand out in any gathering. She was well into some scurrilous story about the upper echelons of the Police Service when Carol called for attention.

"Okay, everyone, settle down. Superintendent Edgar will be here to speak with you shortly, but in the meantime we'll establish the logistics of this investigation, which we're calling for convenience, Operation Pelican."

"Why pelican?" someone asked.

"Because I like them," Carol said. She waited until the room was totally silent before going on. "I know you all have some idea about the scope of this operation, and I want to make it clear that each of us must be careful to keep an open mind, and not fall into the trap of seeing patterns where none may exist."

"There must be a pattern," said Maureen, "otherwise why are we here?" She looked around for a response, but nobody answered.

Carol went on, "It seems to me that there are three possibilities. The first is that there is, indeed, one individual who is responsible for most, if not all, of the deaths we will be investigating. The second possibility is that a copycat element has come into play, so we have different perpetrators using the same method to dispose of their victims. The third possibility is that there is no link between these cases, and that most are accidental deaths or suicides. Incidentally, the post mortem suggests that the Trelawney death at North Head was murder, and not an accident."

She nodded to Bourke to take over. "Please always bear in mind that it's vital that the scope and purpose of the operation be kept entirely confidential," he said. "If these cases are linked, we don't want suspects alerted that they're under investigation. In particular we don't want any media attention at this stage. Any leaks, deliberate or otherwise, will be regarded very severely."

"Don't you trust us, Sarge?" someone called out.

"It's those reporters I don't trust," said Bourke, grinning. "They can wheedle blood out of a stone, so you lot would be easy meat."

He went on to briefly cover the possibility that a murder-for-hire operator had carried out hits in various locations in New South Wales. As he detailed the cases, there were snorts of disbelief and several sarcastic comments, but when Bourke outlined the similarities between them everyone became more serious.

"You'll find in your folder more information on the cases. Not one of them was initially categorized as murder. It's only in hindsight that similarities can be seen. To repeat them: first, cause of death appears to be accidental, or in one case, a suicide; second, apart from the first victim, Paulette Bruehl, in every instance the victim either has existing life insurance increased, or a new policy established a short time before death; third, the beneficiary always, repeat always, has a firm alibi which has been very obviously established with at least one reliable witness. You'll note that the exact time is pointed out to the witness, often more than once."

"So someone's been coaching them," said Miles Li. "But wouldn't there be a worry that this set-up would get noticed, if it kept getting repeated?"

"That's why we're here," said Bourke. "As the cases are spread around different cities, there was a good chance that no one would put two and two together. It was good luck for us and bad luck for the perp that an insurance investigator did happen to notice the recurring pattern."

Carol stepped forward. "What we're looking for is something shared by all these cases. Possible links could include a person or persons in common, participation in the same Internet chatroom or bulletin board, membership in clubs, interests, sports, business contacts — you get the idea. Anything that ties these cases together could lead us to the murderer."

Her audience was now intrigued. Before the questions could start, Carol said, "You are also looking for the money trail — payment from the instigator to the hitman."

"Or woman," Dennis Earl said.

"Oh, very politically correct," mocked Maureen Oatland. "You young guys are something, you know." She leered at Dennis, who looked faintly alarmed at her attention.

Carol said, "As Mark distributes your assignments, you might like to consider how potential clients are located, and how the initial approach would be made. And here's a thought: are there people who've *refused* the offer? These people, if they exist, could be valuable sources of information."

"I'd dispose of anyone who refused the offer," said Anne. "It would be too dangerous to leave them alive."

Superintendent Edgar appeared at the door. "No, don't let me interrupt you." He stood beside Carol, a looming presence, frowning heavily as he watched Bourke hand out the individual responsibilities. When he'd finished, Edgar stepped to the fore, hurumphed loudly, then said,

"All right, men, this could be something big, or" — he broke off to send Carol a challenging look — "a series of coincidences that merely seem to indicate foul play. Whatever, it's up to you to get the data, sift the evidence, get the hard facts. I know I can rely on you all."

He hurumphed again. "And let's play our cards close to our chests, eh? No loose lips on this one, right?"

To Carol he said before he leaving the room, "I want to be kept up to date. The moment anything happens, I need to know, straight away. And no media contacts. I don't want some bloody reporter breaking this story. When, or if, it be-

comes necessary, I'll authorize the information we release."
He shoved his face closer to hers. "My call, Carol. That all
right with you?"

"Fine by me," she said, keeping her face expressionless.

Roham was almost skipping with enthusiasm when he
came to Carol's office for the mandated meeting about his
problem with Bourke. "Operation Pelican," he exulted, "what
a blast!"

"Mark, you and I are here to discuss your complaint about
work allocation," Carol said, attempting to quell him with a
frown.

Roham waved one hand in a forget-it gesture. "Hey, I was
a bit pissed about things, but we cleared it up on Friday night
at the pub."

"From your point of view, how was it cleared up?" Carol
inquired.

A shrug. "Like I needed to get it off my chest, know what
I mean? The Sarge says things will be different now." He sent
a pleased look in Bourke's direction. "And that's okay by me."

"So you're saying the problem's been resolved?"

"Sure it has."

After Roham had bounced out of the room, Carol sighed.
"Hell, Mark, here I am following the human resources hand-
book to the letter, and all Terry Roham needed was a chat
over a beer or two. Simple, really. I can't imagine why I don't
spend more time at the pub solving personnel problems."

The logistics of such a wide-ranging investigation were
daunting. Carol spent the next hours working with Bourke to

streamline the reporting system and to devise a system where the disparate pieces of information about each death could be logged and compared for common qualities.

Earlier in the week she'd decided that she and Bourke would particularly concentrate their efforts on Barry Lyne's death. Since Friday was now set for their drive down to Bulli, and then the few kilometers on to Wollongong, she'd agreed they should take the opportunity to interview Roger Bruehl, whose wife had died at the Gap.

She worked through her lunchtime, wanting to leave reasonably early to spend the evening with her aunt. To-morrow morning she'd be driving Aunt Sarah to the hospital for her operation, then she'd leave and go straight on to the McDonalds' post mortems. There was a certain irony in this juxtapositioning of events. While Dr. Ristow was slicing into Aunt Sarah's body, Jeff Duke would be dissecting Joseph and Faye McDonald.

Mid-afternoon, and almost on a whim, she called Ren Downing and arranged to see him. The office block where Downing & Pate had offices was in the city on George Street. Carol had to admit to herself her visit here was driven more by curiosity than necessity. The building itself was a symphony in shades of blue, from the outside panels through the lobby to the lifts, which featured pale blue beveled mirrors. She found it rather a relief to open the front door of Downing & Pate and find herself surrounded by warmer shades.

She'd imagined that Ren would have had a hand in the interior decoration of the suite, but there was nothing striking in the reception area, apart from a center piece of beautiful flowers on a marble table. The comfortable chairs were up-holstered in dark brown, the thick maroon carpet swallowed her footsteps, the wallpaper was a deep cream with a faint red pattern. It was all rather subdued and reassuringly con-servative, and not at all what she had expected.

The receptionist seated behind a curved rosewood desk got to his feet. "Ren's expecting you, Inspector Ashton. If you'd follow me . . ."

He was, Carol noted, both young and extremely handsome, a male version of the stereotypical leggy blonde in the front office.

"In here, Inspector."

Ren greeted Carol with a hug. "Coffee, Jason, please," he said to the young man, who nodded then vanished, closing the door gently behind him.

This room was also furnished with good taste. Seeing Carol looking around, Ren chuckled. "Expecting something rather more modern and extreme? Perhaps a collage on one wall featuring guns, handcuffs and various accoutrements of law enforcement? Or maybe posters of old gangster movies?"

"Something like that."

He gestured widely. "This is the face of corporate detection, Carol. Our clients want to be reassured, not reminded what a cruel world it is out there. If I had my way I'd be in jeans and a T-shirt reading *Make My Day*, but unfortunately anything like that would go down like a lead balloon."

Jason returned with a tray bearing an elegant coffee pot with matching chinaware. He slid it onto a low table flanked by lounge chairs, then exited as neatly as he'd entered.

Glancing at her watch, Carol reminded herself that this visit was an indulgence. She should be behind her own desk, working hard. "Ren, I'm here to give an unofficial briefing on what's happening. It's for your ears only, but as you brought the cases to our attention, it's only fair that you get an update."

"Your Superintendent Edgar's already called."

Surprised, Carol said, "Edgar called you?"

"Just after you spoke to me. He read me the riot act. The one that says that if I say even one word about these cases

I'll be arrested, drawn and quartered, lose my license, thrown in prison etcetera. I don't take kindly to threats, so we had words."

"Ren, I'm sorry. I had no idea he'd do this."

"Frankly, it seems to me that your super doesn't want to share the limelight. He's sniffed an opportunity to shine, and he doesn't want any competition from me, or anyone else. I'd watch my back, if I were you."

"I always try to."

Handing her a fragile cup, he said, "You'd like it on my side of the fence, Carol. You'd have freedom to act without some arsehole like Edgar second-guessing you every step of the way."

"Thanks for the career advice."

"To change the subject," said Ren, "next Saturday night, are you available? You and your love of the moment? Peter's recently become a gourmet cook, or so he claims, and constantly requires warm bodies to practice his skills upon."

"I'm not sure."

"Get back to me. I'd love to catch up with all your doings — work, lovers, that sort of thing. By the way, who is she, the one you'll bring if you come?"

"It's on a need to know basis," said Carol, amused at his persistence.

"If that's off limits, do what you came for. Tell me what's happening with all those accidental murders."

Carol covered the overall thrust of Operation Pelican, sketched briefly what she'd learned in the Blue Mountains, and gave him the gist of her discussions with Bourke about the logistics of setting up a murder-for-hire business.

"What about Faye and Joseph McDonald? Have you decided it's murder-suicide?"

"The case is only a few days old. We're still investigating." This carefully worded answer seemed to amuse Ren. He cocked his head. "Won't commit yourself, Carol? If you want my opinion, it's a setup, just like the others, and I'll be able to help your inquiries, covertly of course."

Carol raised her eyebrows. "There are policies involved, I know that."

"Callard Assurance is the company in question. We've been retained to look at the situation, as both the McDonalds had million dollar policies."

"Was there a suicide clause?"

Ren nodded approvingly. "No flies on you, Carol, old dear. If Joseph McDonald killed himself, there's no payout on that one. Faye McDonald is another matter."

"So the insurance company wins one, loses one."

"The problem is, I think Callard has lost both of them. I'm betting it was a double murder, not a murder followed by a suicide."

"Follow the money," said Carol. "Penelope Neale gains."

"I've seen her already," said Ren. "She has the alibi down pat." Distaste filled his face. "Strange, cold woman. I took an instant dislike to her." He added playfully, "And you know how I just love everyone."

"Ren, do you really think our hitman is branching out this way? Killing two people and setting the scene up as a murder-suicide takes a great deal more preparation than shoving someone over a cliff."

"Ah," said Ren, "I believe it's the challenge. He's got away with murder several times, and the adrenaline rush has subsided. He needs more, and this is it."

"You think he's a thrill killer, pure and simple?"

"Nothing pure and simple about this one. He's a psychopath having lots of fun and making a profit at the same time. Can't beat it — being happy in your work."

CHAPTER FOURTEEN

The drive to the hospital was a strain, each of them aware they'd said all that could be said for the moment. After the operation there would be much to discuss and arrange, but now words of hope or reassurance sounded hollow. They were both playing parts. Carol assumed a total confidence about the outcome she didn't really have, and Aunt Sarah exhibited a nonchalance Carol knew couldn't possibly be genuine.

The admission procedures at the hospital took time, and small talk was mercifully unnecessary. As Dr. Ristow had described, her aunt, accompanied by Carol, was then taken to have a procedure before the surgery, where, guided by a series of mammograms, a hollow needle was used to insert a wire into the tumor in her breast. This, Dr. Ristow had explained, was to act as a guide during surgery.

After this she was taken to the hospital room where she'd be pre-medicated before the anesthetic. In a pale blue hospital gown, and surrounded by the white sheets of the bed, rather than her usual vibrant choice of colors, Aunt Sarah seemed wan and tired. Carol felt her heart turn over. "Everything will be all right," she said. "It'll soon be over."

"One way or other," said her aunt grimly.

A nurse came in, cheerful but harried. "This will make you a bit woozy," she said, expertly sliding a hypodermic needle into Aunt Sarah's arm. "We'll be along to get you in a few minutes, so just relax."

When she had bustled off, Aunt Sarah said with disgust, "Relax! Not likely."

But Carol could see the injection had already started to work. Her aunt's customary laser green gaze was blunted, and her hands were relaxed. "Darling," she said, slurring a little, "make the right choices, if you can."

"I try."

"You know what I mean. I want you to be happy."

"I am."

This got a gentle snort. "Not the way you could be, should be." Her eyes closed. "Woozy, that nurse said?"

"It will all be over soon, and when you wake up, Sybil will be here."

Her answer was a gentle snore.

They'd discussed last night how Carol couldn't be sure she'd get back to the hospital when Aunt Sarah would be coming out of the anesthetic. Sybil had volunteered to be there in her place, and Carol had accepted gratefully, although with a twinge of guilt.

* * * * *

Jeff Duke was extravagantly pleased to see her. "You've been deliberately avoiding me, Carol. Why is that?" He didn't require any reply. "The McDonalds," he said with every evidence of enjoyment. He gestured to the stainless steel table where a naked body lay exposed. "I'm just about to start."

Carol no longer needed to steel herself while witnessing a post mortem. It was only with children that her heart trembled. Nevertheless, she had to acknowledge the destruction of people as young as Joseph and Faye McDonald was a pitiful thing.

Carol's presence had made Duke turn off the opera he usually had booming through the stark autopsy room. He began his efficient butchery, starting with Faye McDonald. Carol knew he was going to say it, but still groaned when Duke announced, "Ladies first."

"Who killed whom?" he said, removing Faye McDonald's heart and lungs and handing them to an assistant to be weighed, "that's the interesting thing. Tricky, of course, to be accurate about who died first. Hell — impossible, as you know. And I don't think it matters in this case."

"What do you mean?"

"Liz and one of her team were here this morning. Liz will get back to you, but she's sure as hell that Joseph McDonald couldn't have killed himself the way it was set up." Jeff Duke's bellow of laughter was hardly muffled by the double surgical mask he wore. "The only way the guy could kill himself that way would be if he was an orangutan. His arms weren't long enough. Throws a spanner in the works, doesn't it? So much for the theory of murder-suicide by the husband."

He indicated Faye McDonald's shattered head. "And if you think the situation was reversed, and she killed him, then herself, forget it. Judging by the spread of buckshot, there's no way this young woman blew her own head off, not unless her arms are more than two meters long."

On the way back to the Police Centre Carol called the hospital. Dr. Ristow was still in surgery with another patient. She spoke to the nurse in charge of recovery, and was told her aunt had come through the operation well and was in the process of waking up from the anesthetic.

Last night Aunt Sarah had told her she didn't mind close friends knowing about her operation, now that it was definitely scheduled. "I hate people fussing over me, Carol, you know I do. So do tell Mark and Pat, and Leota, if you like. But make them promise not to make a song and dance about the whole thing."

When she got to the Centre she relayed to Bourke what Jeff Duke had said about the McDonalds, and asked him to contact Penelope Neale for another interview. She then told him about Aunt Sarah's cancer. He looked concerned, and then relieved. "I knew something was going on," he said, "but I was afraid to ask."

"Why? What were you thinking?"

Uncomfortable, he didn't meet her eyes. "I don't know. I thought maybe you were interviewing for another job. Edgar's been riding you lately, and he stymied your promotion, we both know that, so I figured . . ."

"You really are serious about the chance that Ren will offer me a job, aren't you? It isn't going to happen, Mark, and if it did, I wouldn't be tempted."

"Are you sure?"

"Of course I am. Now, get me up to speed with what's happened this morning."

Sybil called her an hour later to say that Aunt Sarah had come out of the anesthetic with flying colors and was already demanding to leave the hospital. "She's seriously miffed that Dr. Ristow left word that he wants to see her on his rounds tomorrow afternoon before he'll sign a release."

"Tell her I'll be by this evening with soothing words and her favorite chocolates."

"Carol, would it be all right with you if I took her home with me for the weekend? I know you're flat to the boards, and I'd be thrilled to have her."

"What does Aunt Sarah say?"

"She's all for it."

Both relieved and irritated with herself for feeling that way, Carol said, "Great. I'll bring the patient down on Saturday morning."

Sybil's house was a perfect place to convalesce. It sat high above an ocean beach, with wonderful views of sand, sea and twin headlands guarding the beach. In her mind's eye Carol could visualize the white crests of the surf rolling in constant rhythm to break upon the beige of the sand, the seagulls calling, the smell of the clean salt air.

Bourke broke into her thoughts to say, "I've tried to get hold of Penelope Neale at Dexterous Unlimited, the company that now the McDonalds are dead is all hers, but she's already left for a long weekend. Some yoga retreat in the Hunter Valley."

"You sure she hasn't skipped?"

"Why would she do that? I'd say she's got everything she wants."

Carol remembered the woman's cool, calculating blue stare. "I wonder how much she's paying for it," she said.

It was early afternoon before she finally got hold of Dr. Ristow. The operation had been successful, and he'd removed the tumor and associated tissue and also five lymph nodes under Aunt Sarah's right arm.

"So far it's looking good," he said, "but I can't be a hundred percent sure until I get the pathology results. I'd like to see you both on Monday, when I'll know more."

Then she worked steadily until almost five, when Leota called. "Just checking in," she said. "The convention ends, thank God, tomorrow evening with a dinner I have to attend, but I've got the whole weekend off, Carol, before I have to report back to Canberra on Monday. I know you're busy, but could you fit in a moment or two with a woman who loves you dearly?"

With a pang, Carol realized she'd completely forgotten Ren's dinner invitation for Saturday night. She gave Leota a brief pen-portrait of Ren and how she'd known him for years. "I didn't commit us, so we don't have to go."

"I'd love to."

"You would?"

"Carol, how often do I meet your friends? Apart from Mark Bourke and your delightful Aunt Sarah, you've kept me in the dark."

"About Aunt Sarah," said Carol, "there's something I must tell you." When she'd finished describing her aunt's ordeal there was silence at the other end of the phone. "Leota? Are you there?"

"My mom died of breast cancer."

"I'm so sorry. I didn't know."

"I'll tell you about it some time."

After she'd rung off, Carol mused about how little she knew about Leota and her life. It was a mutual ignorance, as Carol had hardly been forthcoming about herself either.

She didn't have time to brood about this lack of candor as Superintendent Edgar summoned her to give him an update on progress in Operation Pelican. She made a quick call to Ren, who was delighted that she and Leota would, as he put it, "Grace our humble abode," and then gathered up her papers and went to advise the superintendent the McDonald case was looking more and more like a double murder.

"Oh, for God's sake!" he exclaimed, thoroughly disgusted. "Are we going to re-think every death in the entire state? It seems to me the evidence is flimsy here. I want you to concentrate on cases where we can unequivocally prove something. Not run around making up wild theories."

His displeasure evaporated when Carol told him that she and Bourke would be interviewing witnesses in the Barry

Lyne case. "Excellent, Carol. That's one case that Saul Block wanted an excuse to re-open. I've already spoken to him and told him we'll keep him up-to-date. He's guaranteed full co-operation."

Carol had been relieved to see her aunt had color in her face and was sitting up in bed when she arrived at her hospital room.

Aunt Sarah selected a chocolate from the box Carol had brought. "I've got sixteen staples," she said with some pride. "Ten under my arm and six in my boob."

"That sounds awful," said Carol, screwing up her face. "Do they hurt?"

"They're a bit uncomfortable, but that's not the problem." Aunt Sarah frowned heavily. "I hate sleeping on my back, but I'll have to until the staples come out in ten days or so."

Noticing an arrangement of lush hothouse blooms, Carol said, "Who sent those gorgeous flowers?"

"Have a look at the card."

They were from Leota.

"But I didn't tell her what hospital you were in," said Carol, puzzled.

"She's FBI, darling. You know they can find out anything and everything."

Carol wasn't sure why, but this remark made her uneasy. "Perhaps I did tell her," she said, sure she hadn't.

CHAPTER FIFTEEN

Although measured in kilometers Bulli and Wollongong were not far from Sydney, the Friday traffic was always so heavy that Carol insisted on leaving early. It would take some time to clear the outskirts of Sydney and pick up speed on the road south. They had three interviews set up, with Ken Stevens, Roger Bruehl and Alyce Lyne. Bourke hadn't been able to contact Ian Mure.

As she drew up in front of Mark and Pat's impeccable suburban home, Carol thought how much she admired and valued Mark Bourke, both as a friend and as a colleague. They made a formidable team when interviewing witnesses or suspects. Before an important interrogation they would discuss strategies and tactics. Once it began, the intuitive grasp each had of where the other was going with questions or comments would take over.

"I've got some interesting information," Bourke said when he got into the car. "After you left yesterday I got hold of a cop in Wollongong, Mick O'Hare. Haven't seen him for years, but we go back a long way."

"You asked him about Alyce Lyne?"

"Mick didn't know her, but Roger Bruehl was a different matter. It seems that Bruehl's quite a personality in the area, serving on the local council, raising a lot of money for charities, getting his face in the press for pushing local tourism, that sort of thing. A biggish fish in a small pond. After his wife's death last year, he made a few changes in his life."

"Not funded, I imagine, by the insurance payout," said Carol. "Paulette Bruehl only had a small policy."

"Mick says Bruehl certainly doesn't want for cash. He's moved into a big home in a prime part of the city, and he's married again. Caused quite a lot of talk. And you'll never guess who his new wife is."

"I give in. Who is it?"

"Paulette's younger sister, Nicola. Apparently she's quite a looker, and Mick said there'd been rumors Bruehl was carrying on an affair with her behind his wife's back. And there's more . . ."

Carol glanced over to him with a grin. "Oh, cut the dramatic pause, Mark. What is it?"

"Paulette and Nicola Coombes, as they were then, grew up in Wentworth Falls in the Blue Mountains."

"That *is* interesting. The sisters wouldn't have known Alyce Lyne or her brother, would they?"

"Well, here comes the really fascinating bit. Bruehl's in the process of setting himself up as a consultant for local development and tourism, and guess who his partner is, Carol."

"Ian Mure."

"Bingo," said Bourke.

He'd also asked O'Hare to check out Ken Stevens, Alyce Lyne's alibi witness, and had got a call back from the Wollongong detective at home last night.

"We already knew that Stevens had never been arrested, but Mick told me that he had run with a bunch of guys who were later convicted of stealing cars, stripping them and selling the parts. At the time Stevens was a mechanic working part-time at a local garage, so the cops were pretty sure he was involved. Nothing came of it though."

"Isn't he still working at the garage?"

"Yes, but Mick says he owns it now."

"Does he?" said Carol. "Not bad for a part-time mechanic."

"I've left a message for Anne to take a look at Ken Stevens' financial situation," said Bourke. "Wouldn't it be nice if he had a windfall just after Barry Lyne left us for a better place?"

An hour and a half later Ken Stevens was answering the question about his finances himself. Standing on the stained concrete driveway of the little service station, he rubbed his greasy hands on an even greasier rag. "Yeah, I bought this place," he said. "Had a big win on the ponies."

"The local races?" inquired Bourke.

"Nah, Sydney." Stevens looked to Carol, then back to Bourke. "What's goin' on? Thought you was just here about the Blue Mountain thing."

He was an unprepossessing figure, with sharply sloping shoulders, a concave chest, and a weak chin. His straw-colored hair was uncombed. He hadn't shaved. His overalls, once white, were stained and stiff with grease and dirt.

"We are here about the Blue Mountain thing, Mr. Stevens," said Carol agreeably. "Perhaps we could go inside and continue our discussion."

He looked at her warily. "I've got work to do."

"We'll be as quick as possible."

Hunching his narrow shoulders, he led them into the

service station office, a small space into which was crammed a desk covered with a jumble of papers, various vehicle parts, used polystyrene cups and the remains of a fast food breakfast. It was occupied by a weedy young man, wearing overalls almost as filthy as Stevens', who hastily slammed down the phone, picked up his cigarette, and scuttled off.

"Slack bastard," mumbled Stevens, looking after him.

Clearing a space for Carol, he advised, "Can't spare much time. I'm flat out, keepin' up with the work."

He took the other available seat, a creaky office chair. Bourke was left standing.

When Carol asked Stevens to go over his meeting with Alyce Lyne the morning her husband died, he scowled. "Shit, I've been through this a million times."

"Let's try a million and one," said Bourke.

Stevens looked surprised at Bourke's hard tone, then apprehensive. "Okay, okay."

He rattled off his account of how he'd woken up early and decided to go for a stroll. He'd seen a woman pull up and park on Govetts Leap Road near the lookout, and had struck up a conversation with her. They'd talked for some time. She'd mentioned she was there to meet her husband after his run, and she was wondering where he was. Stevens had walked with her down to the lookout, but they couldn't see anything. She'd then said she was terribly worried and asked him to stay with her while she went back to her car and used her mobile phone to call the police. Stevens had waited until they arrived, given his name, then gone back to the bed-and-breakfast where he was staying. Later that day the police had taken him to the station and he'd given a formal statement.

Carol was having a hard time imagining Alyce Lyne spending any time chatting to a specimen like Ken Stevens.

"What did you talk about?" she asked.

"What?"

"You and Ms. Lyne — what did you discuss during this long conversation?"

"I dunno. Things." He stroked his jaw, then brightened up to say, "The scenery. The Blue Mountains. We talked about that."

"Had you been in the Blue Mountains area before this?"

"Nah."

"So what decided you to stay there?"

He ventured a smile. "Seemed a good place to go."

Bourke leaned over Stevens to say, "Do you know Ian Mure?"

Stevens mouth opened, then closed. "Who?"

"Ian Mure," said Carol pleasantly. "Do you know him?"

Stevens shook his head. "Don't think so."

Carol said, "Had you met Alyce Lyne before this particular morning when her husband died."

"No."

There was no hesitation this time, Carol noted.

"She's moved to the Wollongong area. Have you met her since the inquest?"

He licked his lips. "Haven't seen her."

Stevens twisted his head to look up at Bourke, who'd moved behind him. Bourke gave him a tight, menacing smile, then bent down to say, "I'm interested in that money you claim to have won on the Sydney races. With a bookie on the course, was it?"

"Yeah, that's right."

"Big win like that, you'd remember all the details."

"Look," said Stevens, making an attempt to take back some control, "You told me on the phone you wanted to talk about what happened at Govetts Leap, and I've told you all I know. I'm sorry the bloke's dead, but he is. Like, it's old news, it's over."

His face stern, Bourke said, "It's not over, Stevens, when there are new questions about what happened that morning Barry Lyne fell to his death."

The chair gave a protesting squeak as Stevens shoved it

back and got to his feet. "I've nothin' more to say to you. I'm behind with me work, so gotta get goin'.' "

"Did you notice," said Carol to Bourke as they drove towards Wollongong, "that Stevens repeated almost word for word the original statement he gave to the police that morning?"

"Almost as though he memorized it," said Bourke. "I think Mr. Stevens needs to stew for a bit, and then we'll ask him some more questions. He is, as they say, the weak link. I think he'll break when we apply more pressure."

"Can you see him killing Barry Lyne?"

"No way," said Bourke. "He wouldn't have the guts. But if Alyce asked to do her a favor, and paid well for it, he'd agree in a flash."

Roger Bruehl had glossy, minimalist offices in the top floor of a small building in Wollongong's business district. He was tall, slightly overweight, but sleek and well-groomed. There was a touch of gray in thick dark hair and his face was lightly tanned to present a contrast with his very white teeth.

"Come in, come in," he said, shaking hands first with Carol and then with Bourke. "Take a seat. How can I help you?"

Apparently not expecting an immediate answer, he went behind his large desk, sank into the high-backed chair, folded his hands on the leather surface in front of him, and favored them both with a genial, I'm-here-to-be-of-assistance expression.

Most people become uncomfortable with silence in such a situation, and are impelled to fill it with words, so Carol waited for Bruehl to say something. Bruehl, however, seemed quite relaxed and showed no inclination to speak.

Round one to you, thought Carol. "I believe Sergeant

Bourke mentioned when he made this appointment that we had some further questions about the death of your wife last year."

He bent his head to look at his clasped hands. "Yes, Inspector, Paulette's death was a tragic accident, as you know. I still have trouble believing she's gone."

"You've married again," said Bourke.

Bruehl gave him a long hard look. "I don't believe that's any of your business."

"In our work," said Carol with a trace of regret in her voice, "we often find we have to intrude into what would normally be private matters."

A suggestion of impatience crossed Bruehl's face. "I'm sure you're as busy as I am, Inspector Ashton, so let's get this over with. What exactly is it you want?"

"You're working with Ian Mure."

"Yes, we're partners." He unclasped his hands and put them in his lap. "Where are you going with this?"

"Coincidences," said Bourke.

"I have no idea what you're talking about."

Carol said, "Your first wife died after falling a considerable distance —"

"You don't need to remind me of that. I was there. I saw her body when they brought her to the top of the cliff. It was horrific."

As though he hadn't interrupted, Carol went on, "And Ian Mure's brother-in-law died in a similar fall in the Blue Mountains a month later."

Bruehl snorted contemptuously. "And you think one has anything to do with the other? The only similarity is that they were both dreadful accidents."

"Let's talk about your wife's death for a moment," said Bourke. "At the time she fell you claim you were nearby, where your car was parked."

"I didn't see anything. As luck would have it I was talking with a woman who was walking her dog."

"As luck would have it," repeated Bourke.

Bruehl fixed Bourke with a candid gaze. "Do you smoke, Sergeant? For my sins, I do. That morning I found I had cigarettes, but no matches or lighter with me, and the cigarette lighter in the car wasn't working. As you know, it's a hard addiction to buck, so I just had to have a cigarette. I told Paulette that I was going to look for a local shop that might be open when we saw a woman with her dog. A standard poodle. Paulette went off to look at the view while I asked the woman if she had matches or a lighter with her. That's how we got into a conversation."

He's over-explaining, thought Carol. Liars do that. And the direct eye contact is a give-away too. People telling the truth don't use a frank, trust-me stare.

"And did she?" said Bourke. When Bruehl frowned, he added, "Have matches or a lighter with her?"

"No. She wasn't a smoker. That's what we were talking about. I walked along with her while she was telling me what shops might be open at that early hour." His mouth tightened. "I blame myself for the accident. Paulette must have become dizzy, or gone too near the edge. If I'd been with her, instead of chatting to a stranger . . ." He looked down, shaking his head.

Carol leaned back and considered him. He was smooth, but made the common mistake of giving far too much detail in the area he was fabricating. Carol had read the statement from the witness. Bruehl had certainly had the conversation about needing a light for his cigarette. Carol was now convinced it was an invented excuse to give him an alibi while someone else murdered his wife. The witness had seen no one else, but Bruehl had been walking with her away from the lookout, talking all the time.

"You don't have an ashtray on your desk," she observed.
For the first time Bruehl looked disconcerted.

She raised her eyebrows. "Have you given up smoking?"

"Why, yes. Yes, I have."

Carol waited to see if he would embroider this too. This time, however, he was circumspect, and let his short answer stand.

"How long have you known Ian Mure?" she asked, noticing he looked more comfortable with this question.

"I knew Ian slightly when he lived in the Blue Mountains. Paulette grew up in the area, and she introduced us. Ian was doing good things in tourism in the mountains that I thought could work in Wollongong. Then when he moved here we got together and decided to form a partnership."

There were further questions, none of which challenged Bruehl. He declared that his wife's state of mind on the day she died was excellent, confirmed the insurance policy covering her was a small one, and reiterated it had been a pointless, sad accident.

As he rose to see them out, Carol said, "Your first marriage was happy?"

"Of course."

"So you didn't form a relationship with your sister-in-law until after your wife's death."

A faint flush rose in Bruehl's face. "I certainly did not."

"So any gossip prior to the accident isn't true?"

"Absolutely not! Our shared grief threw us together."

Another rehearsed line, thought Carol.

"We'd like to speak with her."

"Why?"

"Standard procedure," said Bourke smoothly.

"Nicola's away at the moment."

Carol raised her eyebrows. "Really? Where?"

"Visiting friends in Melbourne. I'll arrange for her to contact you when she gets back."

"That would be helpful."

Back in the car, while Carol checked a street directory to locate Alyce Lyne's address, Bourke said, "Was there gossip about Bruehl and his sister-in-law?"

"I've no idea," said Carol. "It seemed to me a nice disquieting note to end the interview with the suggestion that we believed that he had a motive to kill his wife."

CHAPTER SIXTEEN

The woman who opened the front door of the luxurious house stood regarding them gravely for a moment before she spoke. "You're very punctual. Do come in, Inspector Ashton, Sergeant Bourke. We'll go through to the back patio. It's sunny and sheltered from the wind and I've put out refreshments. Please help yourself."

Her voice was an arresting contralto, with just a touch of a rough timbre to it.

Carol had seen photographs of Alyce Lyne in the police file, and knew she was good-looking, but was not prepared for the impact of her in person. She was a little under average height, slim but full-breasted, with heavy chestnut hair and deep brown eyes. Her features were regular, her mouth curved even at rest with a faint, knowing smile.

All these elements were attractive, but it was the aura that surrounded her that had the power to enthrall. It was much more than force of personality or the tricks of personal presentation. It was immediately apparent that Alyce Lyne moved and spoke as one secure in the center of a personal universe, who effortlessly became the focal point of all attention.

"Glory be," Bourke said softly. "The siren and her brother."

"Inspector, Sergeant," said Ian Mure from behind his sister. He ushered them through the front door then shook hands, a quick, definite gesture. "I didn't want Allie to meet with you alone. I trust you have no objection to my being here?

"Not at all," said Carol. "We'd hoped to interview you anyway."

Ian Mure smiled wholeheartedly, his eyes crinkling. "Then you can kill two birds with one stone."

He was loose-limbed, rangy, with a graceful yet very masculine way of moving. He had the same thick chestnut hair and brown eyes as his sister. His face, however, was thinner and harder. To Carol, his charm seemed calculated, rather than natural. Carol remembered Lillian Broadhall's assessment that Ian Mure could convince people that black was white, and green was red.

Carol and Bourke followed brother and sister to the patio, which as promised was sheltered and dappled with sun shining through overhanging trees. A greenhouse took up one side. A long table draped with a crisp white tablecloth held an assortment of fruits, breads and cheeses. Carafes held juices and red and white wines.

Alyce popped a grape into her mouth. "As I said, please help yourself."

Her brother lifted a glass of red wine in an ironic toast. "To you, Inspector. I wish you success."

"Thank you." Carol turned to Alyce, who was standing with her hands loosely linked in front of her. "We met with Ken Stevens this morning."

Alyce raised one birdwing eyebrow. "And why would that be?"

Carol said, "We're re-opening the investigation of your husband's death."

"May I ask why?"

"Information received," said Carol blandly.

Ian Mure laughed. "Ah, the first sighting of an official cliché. And many more to follow, I'm sure."

With a boyish grin he went on, "Now, Inspector, don't be angry with me. It's just that I can't take seriously the idea that there's anything else to know about Barry's unfortunate demise."

"We've spoken with your partner, Roger Bruehl," Bourke said.

"Yes, I know. He called me as soon as you left." Ian Mure chuckled. "You quite put the wind up him. I reassured him there was nothing to worry about."

"And was Mr. Bruehl reassured?" Carol asked.

"He's a bit of a worrywart, old Roger is," said Ian Mure with an indulgent smile, "but I think I set his mind at rest. I must say, though, it puzzles me why you're re-investigating the matter now."

"Just some loose ends," said Bourke.

Alyce Lyne put her hand lightly on his arm. "Sergeant, surely you'd like something to eat or drink?" She tilted her head to indicate the laden table. "After all, I have gone to all this trouble . . ."

"No, thank you all the same."

"Ms. Lyne," said Carol, "I wonder if I might be frank?"

She gave Carol a delightful, luminous smile. "Of course, Inspector, be as frank as you like."

How easy it would be for someone to be disarmed by this woman, who used her physical beauty and potent charisma to such great effect.

Carol said, "Speaking bluntly, after meeting Ken Stevens today, I find myself wondering why you spent so much time with him that morning."

"True, he's not Alyce's type," said her brother, "but she's often too soft with needy individuals." He put his arm around his sister to give her a half-hug. "You'll have to toughen up, Allie my dear. Stop letting people take advantage of you."

Carol ignored his comments, looking interrogatively at his sister. "Ms. Lyne?"

"Ken Stevens seemed lonely, Inspector. At the time I was so concerned about Barry, I only half-listened. I could have broken off the conversation at any time, but there's no point in being cruel, is there?"

"And you had never met Stevens before that morning?"

"Never."

"Have you contacted him since?"

"Inspector!" she chided. "Do I look like someone who'd go slumming?" She bit her lip. "How unkind of me. Please forget that I said that."

Carol glanced over at Bourke, guessing he was aware, as she was, that Ian Mure and his sister were enjoying themselves playing with these two cops who'd had the temerity to ask them questions. A certainty, intense and indisputable, possessed her. She hadn't a single doubt Alyce Lyne and Ian Mure had been instrumental in Barry Lyne's death. But proving it was another matter.

"I spoke with Owen Ingram a few days ago," Carol said, "and he admitted covering up the abuse in your marriage."

Alyce clasped her hands. "Oh, poor Owen. Will he get into

very much trouble? I should never have asked him to cover for me, even if he was an old friend."

"Rather more than a friend, I gather."

Alyce sighed. "Did he say that? It isn't true. He's cast me in some erotic private fantasy of his." She gave a little shudder of revulsion. "And I never even knew."

"If your husband was beating you," said Bourke, "then you had every reason to want to be rid of him."

"It wasn't that serious."

"No?" said Carol. "I was told there were black eyes, bruises, a broken rib..." As she spoke, she saw Ian Mure's eyes narrow, and a muscle jump in his cheek.

His voice, however, showed no tension as he interposed, "There was only one serious incident. You should know that when Allie told me what had happened, I got involved. When Barry was sober you couldn't get a nicer guy, but once he got stuck into the alcohol, it was Jekyll and Hyde. I talked some sense into him to the point where he promised to stop drinking, get treatment, join AA, all that sort of stuff. And Barry was all set to do that, when..." His expression was a nice blend of regret and resignation to the vagaries of fate.

"When he died," said Bourke.

"Yes, Sergeant, when he died."

"Mr. Lyne had increased his life insurance shortly before his fall," said Carol.

"As had I," said Alyce. "It was a joint decision that we both carry more insurance. We were planning to have children very soon. Barry and I felt it was prudent."

They had all the answers, Carol thought. It was a game to them — a diverting afternoon's entertainment.

She said, "Do either of you happen to be acquainted with Joseph and Faye McDonald?"

There was the merest flicker of something on Ian Mure's face. Surprise, perhaps. Not apprehension.

Alyce shook her head. "I don't think so. Ian, do you know them?"

"I meet so many people. It's a common name. There could be a McDonald in there somewhere. I can't recall at the moment. Is it important, Inspector Ashton?"

"They were partners with Penelope Neale in a company called Dexterous Unlimited. Perhaps you know Ms. Neale?"

Ian Mure shook his head. "Sorry, that's not a familiar name." He smiled engagingly. "Of course, I meet so many people . . ."

Carol signaled to Bourke that they should leave. "Thank you for your time," she said formally.

Alyce frowned. "You're not going, Inspector, without having something to eat or drink?"

"I'm afraid we must."

They were escorted to the door as if they were honored guests, then brother and sister waited politely side by side as Carol and Bourke got into their car.

"Jesus," said Bourke, "it's Ian Mure. I know that as surely as I know my own name. But we'll never prove it."

"I think it's the two of them, Mark, working together."

As she started the car she glanced at Ian and Alyce, still standing at the front door. They made a golden pair, secure in their power to control their domain. "They're clever, intelligent psychopaths."

"The worst kind," said Bourke, with a small smile.

"I'm speculating their first victim may have been their elder brother when they were still at school. Lillian Broadhall said he fell under a train, but she wouldn't be drawn as to whether it was a genuine accident or not."

"I'll pull the records. There would have been an inquest, and the Railways would have done their own investigation too."

"While you're at it," Carol said, "check if anyone they were associated with died or was injured in a fall. Cover the period from high school right up to the present."

"You're thinking there may have been a practice accident?"

"I think there's a good chance there was."

"Alyce is so bloody beautiful," said Bourke, "I'd think she could get anything she wanted without killing for it."

"You know your criminology, Mark. These two are charming, remorseless psychopaths. They mimic the behavior of normal, caring individuals so well that most people are completely taken in. But they don't feel like us. They have no guilt and very little fear. In their own eyes, they're invincible. And manipulating others is a game to them — we're chess pieces to be moved on their board."

Bourke looked morose. "If we don't stop this lot, they'll keep on keeping on." He leaned back and folded his arms. "What do you think they'll do next?"

"Now that they're aware we have suspicions and will continue asking questions, to protect themselves they're going to start looking for that weak link you mentioned. Ken Stevens is one, and maybe Roger Bruehl. In fact, from Ian and Alyce's point of view, any of their former clients are potential liabilities."

"They're not going to start a wholesale slaughter, Carol. That would be too obvious."

"I agree. If I were Ian and Alyce, I'd execute a former client as an example to the others, to make sure they kept their mouths shut." She laughed without much humor. "Hell, Mark, I believe I'm beginning to think like them!"

CHAPTER SEVENTEEN

Carol had brought Aunt Sarah home from the hospital late on Friday afternoon. She'd said she felt fine, but looked exhausted. Carol had ignored her protests it was too early to go to bed, and had settled her down in the guest room. When Carol had come back with tea and biscuits, Aunt Sarah had been sound asleep.

On Saturday morning, Carol was still concerned, anxiously watching her aunt's painful progress up the path to the carport, preceded by Sinker, his tale erect. Carol's offer of a supporting arm had been rejected, although she had been allowed to carry the overnight bag.

"Aunt Sarah, you're pushing it. Sybil will understand, so why not stay here for the weekend?"

"You're working darling, aren't you?"

"Yes, a lot of the time, but —"

"I'd rather be down at the beach with Sybil. And if Yancey's there, she's promised to do the preliminary sketches for my portrait."

"Your portrait? And who's Yancey?"

Aunt Sarah looked as though she regretted bringing up the subject. "It's nothing dear. Just a whim of mine." Her enthusiasm rising, she couldn't resist adding, "I'll be portrayed as an Eco-Crone, with the unspoiled environment behind me. Sort of a heroic figure."

Bemused by this vision, Carol shooed Sinker back into the garden, helped her aunt into the car, put the overnight bag in the boot, and slid into the driver's seat.

"This Yancey is an artist?"

"She is." She cast a severe look at Carol. "I don't want to talk about my portrait. I shouldn't have mentioned it in the first place. Let's drop the subject."

They chatted about inconsequential things on the run to the coast, passing bushland edging Wakehurst Parkway that was regenerating from fierce summer fires. It always gave a lift to Carol's spirits to see the green springing from blackened eucalyptus trees that had burned like torches in the conflagration, and been left as sooty skeletons. After a bushfire the first rains acted like a magic potion, causing new life to spring from the blackened soil and shoots to appear on the bare branches.

Sybil, wearing white canvas pants and a dark green top that made her red hair flame in contrast, met them as Carol pulled into the drive. The house above them, reached by a flight of steep stone steps, had an enviable view of the surfing beach. Looking up, Carol caught sight of someone at the front door. She felt uncomfortable, and was furious with herself for feeling that way.

"Are you coming in, Carol?" Sybil asked as she helped Aunt Sarah from the car. "Please do. I've got croissants from the local bakery. You know how great they are."

"Sorry, I can't. I've got to go into work."

Sybil smiled. "Next time, then." Picking up Aunt Sarah's bag, she said to her, "I'll take you in through the garage. The stairs are easier that way."

Carol kissed Aunt Sarah's cheek. "I'll see you Sunday night. Look after yourself and don't overdo it."

She was about to open her car door when the woman who'd been at the front door came down the steps, held out her hand, and said, "I'm Yancey."

"Carol."

Maintaining what she hoped was a polite, not-too-interested expression, Carol said, "You're painting Aunt Sarah's portrait, I hear."

"I hope to. She's a wonderful subject." Giving Carol and appraising look, she added, "You would be, too."

"Thank you," said Carol, assessing her in turn. Yancey was of medium height, full-figured, with brown hair, brown eyes and a generous mouth. One crooked front tooth gave her smile a fillip.

Sybil came lightly down the steps. "I've got Aunt Sarah installed meekly in a chair, but I know she's going to be a handful. She's already talking of a walk on the beach."

Carol laughed, said goodbye, and climbed into her car. As she drove away she deliberately didn't look in the rear view mirror.

"I vote we remove Ursula Stein from the list," said Bourke. He'd picked up fresh pastries and two coffees on the way in, and the smells mingled delightfully in Carol's office.

As it was the weekend, he hadn't worn his usual suit and tie, but blue jeans, spotless sneakers and a long-sleeved top of such pristine whiteness that Carol was forced to say, "How do you keep so clean, Mark? Don't you ever dribble coffee down your front?"

"Never," he said with equanimity. "Now, how about dropping the Ursula Stein case? Nanette's done a good job uncovering two previous suicide attempts in Germany, both made before she met her husband, and apparently concealed from him. That makes Ursula Stein's death much more likely to be a successful suicide, and not murder."

"Okay, take her off the list. Is there anyone else we can remove?"

"Not really, but I think we should focus on the cases that look most promising."

Carol considered the names. "Obviously after yesterday we know we have to concentrate on Paulette Bruehl and Barry Lyne. I'd add Captain Trelawney, because it's so recent, and also Joseph and Faye McDonald because that's where the murderer had to take the most risks. You've seen Liz Carey's report. She was right about it not being a suicide. McDonald couldn't have held the shotgun at that angle and fired it without using an extension to reach the trigger, and there was nothing like that at the scene."

After discussion, Carol and Bourke decided to re-deploy some of the team. "Anne is very good to do with anything involving financial matters," said Bourke. "I'll set her on the money trail. She's already looking into Ken Stevens' windfall win at the track. She can do the Trelawney and McDonald cases too, but first I'll have her check out Alyce and Ian's finances, because somewhere they're concealing a lot of dollars. That is, presuming these hits were done for money, not love."

"Mark," said Carol, struck with what he'd said, "I'd wager there were at least two hits that weren't made for money. What if Paulette Bruehl's death was a favor to her husband, so he could marry her younger sister? And for this Ian Mure got a partnership with Roger Bruehl?"

"And of course," said Bourke, "Brotherly love alone led Ian to kill Barry Lyne. I'm sure you noticed his reaction when you mentioned the results of the beating Alyce's husband gave her."

They worked for another hour establishing the best system to collect and make sense of the large amount of data that would be coming in from different investigations. When they had finished, Bourke stretched, then sat back with his hands behind his head.

"You know," he said, "now that I've met the Lethal Two, I don't have nearly as much trouble understanding how they could recruit clients."

"I agree," said Carol. "They're both expert in reading human frailties and taking advantage of them."

Bourke gazed at the ceiling, musing. "For my money, we're going to find that many of these contracts to kill came about through personal recommendations. 'You hate your husband?' says a friend or acquaintance. 'Maybe I know someone who can do something about it.' And then Ian or Alyce get in touch."

"I see these as MAD situations," said Carol. "Mutual Assured Destruction. In each case, both the client and the killer go down if either one talks."

"We both know some people, when they get away with murder, just can't help boasting about it to someone," said Bourke, "even if the hit it was a secondhand thrill, with a hired killer to do the deed."

"I know what I'd do," Carol said, imagining herself a murderer for hire. "I'd record every conversation between me and the client, on the phone or face to face. Plus I'd keep copies of any communications via the Internet."

Bourke sat up. "Very self-incriminating, Carol."

"But think what security you're giving yourself, Mark. And you can disguise your voice with an electronic device, so a voice print can't identify you. After the murder is carried out, the client thinks, 'Why should I pay more? It's done, and the killer can't say anything without being arrested himself.

If he tries to implicate me, I'll say I know nothing about it, or that the idea was a joke that I never meant to be taken seriously.' "

"So it's a bit of a shock," said Bourke, "when the copies of those damning conversations arrive in the mail."

"Exactly," said Carol. "Particularly if the murderer advises that the originals are somewhere secure, and tells the client — it doesn't have to be true — that, 'If anything happens to me my lawyers have a sealed envelope that will be forwarded to the police.' "

"I like it, Carol. And as a bonus you have the potential of a little blackmail down the line."

"I'd make a master criminal," she said with satisfaction. "Good thing I'm not turning to the dark side . . ."

Carol had taken a change of clothes with her, so she went straight to Leota's hotel when she left the Police Centre. "Carol," said Leota, opening the door wearing a terry toweling bathrobe, "you need a shower."

"I do? I had one this morning."

"That one was for cleanliness. Now, *this* one is for something else altogether."

Laughing, Carol allowed herself to be led in the direction of the bathroom.

Much later, cleaner and satisfyingly satiated, Carol relied on past memory to find Ren and Peter's house. They lived in Alexandria, an inner city suburb whose fortunes had risen over recent years as professionals with money had moved in to alter, refurbish and extend the original working class homes.

After a couple of false turns she finally found the correct street. The house itself she remembered clearly, a charming little cottage in a row of similarly charming cottages, each featuring some individual touch that personalized the dwelling. Ren and Peter's had a magnificent leadlight panel in the front door which Leota was commenting upon when Ren opened it, smiling widely.

"Carol! And Leota! Come in."

"We were admiring your door," Leota said.

"The leadlight was salvaged from some mansion being demolished for a block of flats." He took her arm. "Now, come right along with me, Leota. All I know is your name, and a delightful one it is. Carol would tell me nothing more, so I'm consumed with curiosity."

Over his shoulder he said to Carol, "Sweetstuff, why don't you go and give Peter a hand. It's crisis time in the kitchen."

As they disappeared into the living room Carol heard Leota say, "Sweetstuff? You get away with calling Carol, *Sweet-stuff*? You're clearly quite a man."

She found Peter frowning into an space-age oven in a kitchen that would not seem out of place in a restaurant. "Carol! Long time no see." They embraced for a moment, then Peter was back at the oven tut-tutting to himself. "They never get the time right in recipes," he said. "This should be cooked, and it isn't."

He'd put on some weight since Carol had seen him last, and lost some hair. He'd grown a droopy mustache. She generally didn't like facial hair on men, but it rather suited him.

Peter handed her a glass of red wine — "Cooking wine, but pretty good stuff." He had her sit on a high stool. As he ricocheted around the kitchen, she perched there sipping wine and chatting with him about people they both knew. She felt relaxed, welcomed, at ease.

Perhaps, she thought, I should start having dinner parties again. I haven't bothered since Sybil left . . .

She surprised herself by saying, "You know everyone, Peter. Has an artist named Yancey ever crossed your path?"

"Yancey Blake? Oh, yes, she's very well known. Does a lot of portraits. Highly regarded." He raised an eyebrow. "Painting you, is she?"

"No, actually it's my aunt who's the subject."

He disappeared into the walk-in pantry, muttering to himself about spices. When he reappeared he said, "Ren tells me you and Sybil have parted ways."

"That's true."

Peter grinned at her. "You don't need to use that tone with me, Carol. I'm not a professional stickybeak like Ren, you know." He made a cut-off gesture. "End of personal questions. Unless, of course, there's something you're just burning to tell me . . ."

"I lead a very boring life."

"Not at the moment, surely. Ren says he's been talking to you about a serial killer."

Carol wasn't happy to hear this. On her part she hadn't mentioned anything at all about Operation Pelican to anyone outside work, not even in the most general terms. Hell, she hadn't even told Leota, who, after all, was in law enforcement too. "What's Ren been telling you?"

Peter cocked his head. "Do I detect a frosty note in your voice? There's no need, Inspector Ashton, Ma'am. Not only am I sworn to secrecy, frankly, Ren hasn't really told me much at all. Besides, who am I going to spill it to? The kids?" He was a primary school teacher, who spent his working days with several hundred students under the age of twelve.

"Why's it so important to keep it quiet?" he asked. "Are you about to spring the trap?" Peter illustrated trap-springing by slapping his hands together and exclaiming, "Gotcha!"

"I wish."

A timer rang. "Good grief," said Peter, leaping in the direction of the stove, "I'm not ready for the vegetables to be ready."

Carol sipped her wine and thought about Peter's question. Before they had viable suspects, there had been every reason to keep the fact that murder cases across the state were connected. Now that she and Bourke were incontrovertibly sure that they had identified the two principals in the murder-for-hire scheme, then judicious leaking of information to the media could be of use.

It was a slim to none chance that Ian Mure and Alyce Lyne would crumble under pressure, but there were others involved who might be susceptible. Ken Stevens, in particular, would eventually crack, and Carol felt sure Owen Ingram too, knew more than he had admitted to her.

It was a lovely evening, full of laughter, good food, and companionship. Carol successfully banished from her thoughts her problems at work, worries about Aunt Sarah, questions about where her relationship with Leota might be going, and lastly, the puzzling response Carol had to something that should be pleasing — the fact Sybil was getting on with her life.

By one in the morning, everyone, with the exception of Carol, who'd stopped drinking earlier because she was driving, was pleasantly tipsy. There were several loud goodbyes, anxious shushings and muffled laughing, but finally Carol got Leota into the car.

"Terrific evening," said Leota as they drove off. "I like your friends. Most fun I've had for ages." She yawned, then put her head on Carol's shoulder.

Carol knew she shouldn't bring up the subject now, but she did, anyway. "Leota, those were lovely flowers you sent Aunt Sarah, but why didn't you call me and ask the name of the hospital?"

Leota sat up and looked at her. "Excuse me? Am I missing something here?"

"You used FBI resources to find out where Aunt Sarah was, didn't you?"

Leota peered at her as if she'd grown two heads. "I rang around the hospitals to find out where your aunt was a patient. You're telling me you've got a problem with that?"

"I have," Carol admitted, "but I'm not sure why."

"Maybe you're thinking that I might spy on *you*. Is that it? Find out things you didn't want me to know?"

"Of course I don't think you'd do that." To lighten the conversation she wished she'd never started, Carol added, "Anyway, you wouldn't find anything of interest. My life is an open book."

"An open book? Can that be true?"

"Well," said Carol, "more or less."

After a long pause, Leota said, "I could be called back to the States any time. You know that."

Carol kept her eyes on the road. "Let's not talk about it now."

"We need to discuss the future." Leota gave a rueful laugh. "Carol, we need to discuss if we *have* a future."

"I'm tired, Leota."

"Be honest with me. Could you see yourself living in the States?"

"Maybe. I haven't thought seriously about it."

"I think we should both give the subject some serious thought."

Carol glanced across at her. "Have you heard you're being recalled?"

"No." Leota sighed. "Lousy timing, Carol. Forget it. We can discuss it later."

They began to chat about the evening, but underneath their light conversation Carol felt the tension of an unspoken word. Commitment.

CHAPTER EIGHTEEN

"I was called at home," snapped Superintendent Edgar. "At home!" He paused to let the enormity of this sink in. "Asked me point blank if we were investigating a series of murder-for-hire cases. Mentioned Operation Pelican by name. How in the hell would Vida Drake get my number? It's not listed." He glared at Carol as though she must have the definitive answer.

"Vida Drake's an investigative reporter. She has contacts. She can get any number she wants, just the way we can."

His face folded into angry lines, Edgar barked, "Don't give me that, Carol. This Drake woman's onto the fact we're investigating murder-for-hire. There must be a leak in your team."

Having had a strenuous weekend with not a lot of sleep, Carol was far from a placatory frame of mind. "If there's a leak, it hasn't come from my side."

"Really? Then where?"

After Carol had pointed out that there were literally dozens of people, from the Commissioner's office down, who knew something about Operation Pelican, he waffled for a moment, then conceded she was right. "So what are we going to do about it?" he demanded.

"I believe some media attention could be useful at this point."

"It's too early. We need something definite to show we're on top of it." He made his habitual grooming gesture, running his hand over his thick white hair. "An arrest, Carol, would be nice."

"We need evidence."

"Evidence, yes." He slapped his heavy hand on the Carol's last report, which she'd left on his desk late Sunday afternoon. "This brother and sister team, you're absolutely sure it's them? Coincidences, I remind you, do happen."

"Not this many," said Carol. "Although unfortunately, coincidences aren't hard evidence. That's why I'm suggesting that you might consider a controlled leak. It'll put pressure on potential witnesses on the periphery, people who know something, but aren't so involved that they'll land themselves in jail if they come forward."

A thoughtful expression was followed by, "The Commissioner wants to see us this morning. He's demanding to be brought right up to date. This controlled leak idea, let me try it out on him. If he doesn't put the kibosh on it, then I'll consider the proposition."

Carol translated this to mean that if the Commissioner liked the idea, Edgar would take credit for it. However, if the Commissioner didn't give a positive response, then the idea would be all Carol's.

Shuffling papers on his desk, the superintendent

eventually came up with budget projections for the department. "Now Carol, you know we've been asked to pull in our belts a bit," he said. "We have to do more with the allocation we've got. That means we can't follow these two suspects around waiting for something to happen. We haven't got the manpower, Wollongong hasn't got the manpower. And anything above normal overtime will blow our budget projections. You'll have to do the best with the resources you've got. And keep an eye on travel costs. I don't want wild goose chases all over New South Wales."

"Mark Bourke's traveling to the Blue Mountains this morning. You'll see I mention in my report that a teacher died in a fall during the time Ian and Alyce Mure attended the school. Mark's checking that, and also the death of the elder brother in the family."

"Right, right." He made an irritable gesture, brushing away these petty details. "Keep me posted, and if that Drake woman approaches you, you're to tell me immediately."

The waiting room at Dexterous Unlimited had randomly arranged panels in primary colors on the walls, a carpet with a zigzag pattern, and hanging from the ceiling an aviary full of mechanized birds, brightly-feathered and designed to open their artificial beaks, flutter, squawk, stretch their wings, and in general mimic real creatures. They provided a constant background noise of twittering that was beginning to get on Carol's nerves.

Carol and Roham had come in separate vehicles because the new industrial park where Dexterous Unlimited was situated was an easy drive from Carol's house. She'd go straight from here to pick up Aunt Sarah at home and take her to the appointment with the surgeon to get the verdict on the operation's success.

Carol glanced at Terry Roham. With Bourke absent, she

had decided to give Roham an opportunity to participate in a key interview, even if only to take notes. Roham was plainly nervous, running his hand over his short, curly hair, clearing his throat, and checking that his tie was straight.

"I ask the questions, you take the notes," said Carol.

He nodded. "Okay."

The receptionist, a young woman so listless it seemed an effort for her to breathe, wandered over to where they were sitting. "Ms. Neale just rang through. She'll see you in her apartment." She raised a languid hand to point. "You have to go out the front here, then around to the left and up the metal stairs to her private entrance."

Outside, the air was cool, with a bite of the winter to come. As she always did, Carol assessed her surroundings. The industrial park was made up of a series of squares, with three-story buildings lining the sides. A broad street led into each square, and narrower alley-ways ran on each side of the individual buildings. They were modern, utilitarian structures, with loading docks a standard feature. Extensive landscaping featuring leafy bushes had been employed to soften the sterile lines.

The Dexterous Unlimited structure stood out because of the bright colors of each floor — red, yellow, blue — and for the fact that greenery showed at the edge of its top floor, where a roof garden flourished.

As the receptionist had indicated, a broad iron stairway was attached to the side of the building, each flight corresponding with the color of the story. Carol and Roham mounted the steps, the first flight red, then yellow, and lastly a particularly bright blue. At the top was a black door that opened as they gained the landing. "Come in," said Penelope Neale.

It was a surprisingly attractive apartment, furnished with expensive furniture and lit with natural light from skylights.

Sliding doors opened into an extensive roof garden, filled with greenery.

"I chose to live here, in the company building," said Penelope Neale. As if Carol had voiced a criticism of this, she added quickly, "I prize the isolation, if you can understand that, Inspector."

She wore neutral colors, camel slacks and a cinnamon pullover. She had scraped her pale hair back into a ponytail, and her sallow face seemed stretched by this into a mask. As before, her startling eyes flashed blue fire.

"That's beautiful," said Carol, again noticing the silver ring on Penelope Neale's little finger.

She glanced down at her hand, then began to turn the ring around, as though she could screw it on more tightly. "I've had it since I was a child. My mother gave it to me.' Her thin lips twisted as she added, "It's the only gift I can remember from her."

What a lifetime of resentment was contained in those words, Carol thought. But resentment enough to pay to have your only sister blasted with a shotgun?

"Thank you for seeing us, Ms. Neale. This is Detective Constable Roham. He will be taking notes of our meeting."

Penelope Neale seated them in an area that looked out onto the roof garden. Carol said, "You practice yoga?"

"What?" She licked her lips. "Why are we talking about that?"

"You had a long weekend in the Hunter Valley."

"I find it relaxing. Now can we get on? I want to know when the inquest will be held." Sitting stiffly in her chair, she avoided looking directly at Carol. "You understand, Inspector, I never expect to entirely recover from Faye's death. In my nightmares I still relive that dreadful scene in the kitchen. However, it's important that I achieve some sort of closure."

As she had in the first interview, Carol felt the woman was

reading rehearsed lines that were intended to convey what would be expected from a bereaved sister. She glanced over at Terry Roham, who was frowning at his notebook, wondering if he were sensitive enough to detect the facile quality of Penelope Neale's words.

"I'm afraid we have a problem establishing when the inquest will be, Ms. Neale."

"A problem?"

"Based on evidence, we no longer consider this a murder-suicide."

Hearing the swift intake of breath, Roham looked up.

"Whatever can you mean?" she demanded. "I discovered them. I saw what Joseph had done."

"It seems very likely it was a double murder," Carol said calmly. "That means we're back at square one, looking for motives."

"I've no idea of motives. No idea at all."

"I'm interested in the insurance policies," said Carol.

Penelope Neale's face was blank of expression. "It's standard for any partnership to have joint insurance. It's good business practice in case something happens to a partner."

"Who was the driving force behind the company?" Carol inquired.

"The three partners were important." She looked down at her hands clasped in her lap. "Important, each in an individual way."

"How were you important, Ms. Neale?"

There was a flush high on her cheekbones. She glared at Carol. "I don't pretend to be creative as far as computer games are concerned. That I left to Faye and Joseph, and their hand-picked staff. I run the financial side of the company. That's my responsibility."

"Do you know Ian Mure, Ms. Neale?"

She blinked, waited a moment too long, then said, "No, I don't think so."

172

"Are you sure you haven't met?"

"I'm sure."

"Perhaps you know his sister, Alyce."

Penelope Neale shook her head emphatically. "No."

Shifting to innocuous questions, Carol waited until she seemed more at ease, then asked, "Do you have any connections to the Blue Mountains region? Perhaps you lived there, visited? Or perhaps you have friends or relatives . . .?"

Penelope Neale sat very still. "I don't believe so."

Carol waited for her to elaborate, but she remained silent, staring at the floor.

After the interview, when they were on their way to the visitors' parking area, Terry Roham said with satisfaction, "She didn't ask why. Dead give-away, if you ask me."

"I'm glad you noticed that."

"Yeah, when you mentioned Ian and Alyce Mure, and the Blue Mountains, she should have asked what this had to do with her sister's murder. But she didn't."

Carol found herself pleased with Roham, an unaccustomed emotion.

It was almost a re-run of the initial appointment with the surgeon. Dr. Ristow hurried in late, apologizing as he rushed through the door. Carol thought, as she had the first time, how his short red hair and mustache didn't quite fit her image of what a surgeon should look like.

He sat down and beamed at Aunt Sarah. "I have to say that the results of your operation are positive, very positive."

"It hadn't spread?" said Aunt Sarah, relief breaking on her face. "Is that what you're saying?"

"We removed what we call the sentinel nodes, the first part of the lymph system where cells from your cancer would take up residence. These nodes were examined very carefully,

173

and they're clear, I'm pleased to say, so I feel confident in stating that the cancer hasn't spread anywhere else in your body."

Carol let out her breath in a long sigh. "Thank God."

"The schedule now," said Dr. Ristow, "is to start radiation treatment under the supervision of Dr. Yeats about one week after the staples come out and you've healed completely. Just to remind you, the radiation is to kill any stray malignant cells that may still be in floating around in your breast. You'll have treatment for seven weeks, every day except for the weekend. Any questions?"

"When do the staples come out?" asked Aunt Sarah. "I'm sick of sleeping on my back."

"Ten, twelve days after your operation. I think that would make it a week from today."

Everything had been explained thoroughly from the beginning, so neither Aunt Sarah nor Carol had much more to ask. Very shortly thereafter they were in Carol's car traveling back to the house at Seaforth.

"I just can't tell you how relieved I feel," Carol said. She looked over at her aunt, who was staring somberly out at the traffic. "What's wrong?"

"I was just thinking how lucky I am to have caught the cancer at Stage One when it's so treatable. And that's thanks to mammograms. I'm never going to complain again about a little discomfort when my breast's squished between those glass plate thingies on the machine. After all, what's a bit of nuisance pain when you compare it to the alternatives, a radical mastectomy or even death?"

She glanced over at Carol with a thoughtful frown.

"Don't start," Carol commanded. "You don't have to bully me. I've already told you I have a mammogram once a year."

"Hmmm," mused Aunt Sarah. "I wonder if every one of our Eco-Crones is as sensible."

Carol had to grin. "I feel a crusade coming on."

CHAPTER NINETEEN

Carol called a team meeting on Tuesday morning to bring everyone up to speed on the recent developments and to explain the re-allocation of duties made necessary now that names could be put to prime suspects.

Anne Newsome reported that tracing a financial tie between Ken Stevens and Alyce Lyne or her brother was impossible, as any transfer of money had obviously been in cash. "There are several large cash withdrawals from both Ian and Alyce's accounts about that time, but no way to prove any of that money was given to Ken Stevens to buy the garage he worked at."

"What's Stevens' present financial position?"

"Not good," said Anne. "He's maxed out his credit cards

and he's clearly going to have trouble paying for the next delivery of petrol."

"Blackmail might be a viable option," said Carol to Bourke.

He grinned. "Only if our Kenny doesn't value his life."

Several others in the team reported on their efforts, including Maureen Oatland, who'd been checking on Dianne Beaton, Captain Trelawney's daughter. "Not what you'd call a stable, well-balanced individual," she said with a mocking smile. "A prickly woman who gets into arguments easily. Things aren't helped by the fact the big house she lives in is mortgaged to the hilt and she's been running late with payments. She really needs that inheritance from her father. Good luck for her it's a substantial estate."

"So Dianne Beaton's in no position to make a large cash withdrawal?" Carol asked.

"I was getting to that," said Maureen. "The month before her father died she used a combination of her many credit cards to make cash withdrawals for a total of ten thousand dollars."

"I think we need to see Ms. Beaton," said Carol.

Bourke reported on his trip to the Blue Mountains. "I spent yesterday afternoon in Katoomba," he began.

"Nice work if you can get it," someone commented.

"As I was saying," said Bourke, "I was forced out of the office by duty, and had an arduous drive through pleasant scenery while you lot were slaving away here. But what I found wasn't pleasant at all. When Ian Mure was a senior at high school he went on an excursion with other students to examine geological features in the area. The teacher who accompanied the group, Mr. Walton, had recently failed Ian Mure on an important exam because of cheating, and had refused to mark key assignments in the subject because he accused Mure of flagrant plagiarism. During this excursion Mr. Walton fell to his death from a walking trail at the edge of a cliff."

"I'm betting Ian Mure was near him."

"If he was, Miles, no one present mentioned it. There was no suggestion at the time that it was anything but an unfortunate accident. Now, it looks like Mure's second successful attempt at a perfect crime."

"Second attempt?" said Nanette. "How old was he when he tried the first?"

"Ian and Alyce's elder brother, a renowned bully who regularly mistreated his younger brother and sister, fell under a freight train when Ian was fourteen and Alyce was seventeen. They were both present at the scene, and later gave tearful evidence at the inquest that their brother was fooling around and fell off the platform into the path of the train. No one suspected them of being involved. In light of their later activities, though, it was possibly their first kill."

After discussion, Carol took over. "I believe Mark is on the right track when he says that most, if not all of these murder-for-hires were arranged by a referral system. That means you are to look for friends, relatives, acquaintances that have some connection in the broad sense with the Blue Mountains region or with the Wollongong area. More specifically, try to uncover links to Ian Mure or his sister, Alyce. Note that people who know Alyce well call her Allie. Other key people would be Roger Bruehl and Nicola Coombes, her name before she married her dead sister's husband. In the most recent case, Trelawney's death at North Head, we're looking for connections with either his widow, Evelyn, or his daughter, Dianne Beaton. Bear in mind that the person providing the referral does not have to figure largely in the client's life. They could have gone to school together, or been employed in the same place."

"Jeez," said Maureen Oatland, "this makes looking for a needle in a haystack seem easy by comparison."

"What if the same person does a lot of referrals?" said Anne Newsome. "He or she acts as a broker for murder."

In the buzz of amusement that followed this suggestion,

Miles Li raised his voice to say, "Cops see people who deserve to be murdered every day, so why not a cop as a broker?"

Carol broke into the laughing comments this caused to say, "The Commissioner has agreed that there should be a controlled flow of information to the media, with the purpose of putting pressure on potential witnesses who might come forward."

"Offer them money," someone suggested. "That'll make them keen."

"No reward will be offered, at least at this point."

She was about to go on, when Bourke touched her arm. "I've got an urgent call. Be back in a moment."

Carol continued with the meeting, emphasizing that fast, accurate reporting to the central information pool, to be run by Dennis Earl under Mark Bourke's supervision, would mean threads that might not be seen by individual investigators could be highlighted when all the data was analyzed.

Bourke came back, a grim expression on his face. "That was Mick O'Hare in Wollongong. Ken Stevens was found dead this morning at his garage, crushed under a car. Apparently the hydraulic jack failed. It looks like Ian and Alyce didn't waste any time getting rid of that particular weak link."

There began a time that Carol always found particularly trying, when data poured in, but no patterns emerged and no firm evidence was discovered. Telephone records were scanned, Internet chatrooms and bulletin boards monitored, financial dealings examined. Payment was clearly not made by any bank transfer, but by cash. Indeed, there were many odd cash withdrawals by presumed clients, but none that could be nailed down as payment for murder.

The death of Ken Stevens was investigated by the Wollongong police, liaising with Bourke, but no evidence of murder was found. The hydraulic jack was, like most of the equipment in the service station, old and badly maintained, so the fact it had failed was quite within the realms of possibility. The certainty was there, of course, that it was murder, but in the absence of any proof of this, the case was about to be closed.

Although there was no hard evidence that would stand up in court, inferences were everywhere: the Hunter Valley yoga ashram where Penelope Neale went for weekend retreats also had Alyce Lyne as an occasional visitor. The husband of Cindy Dunn, who'd died falling down fire stairs, belonged to a model aircraft club that attended meetings with other enthusiasts all over the state, and a cousin of the Mures, Pete Affley, was a member of a similar club in Dubbo. Hilda Perry, who'd drowned in heavy seas near Kiama, had a brother who inherited the entire family estate at her death, and he was active in tourism in the South Coast area, which included Wollongong.

Carol had long meetings with each of the insurance companies who had paid out on the policies, affronting and alarming them all by asking if anyone in their employ, or any insurance agents or brokers using their services, could possibly be involved in setting up the murders. Each insurance company expressed keen interest in the success of the police investigations, hoping to recover the considerable sums they'd paid out. They were much opposed, however, to the suggestion that anyone associated with them might be culpable in any way.

Three weeks passed. Aunt Sarah had her staples removed, and was amused and, Carol thought, rather pleased, to have the radiology staff, after careful measurement, tattoo tiny marks on her breast to guide the radiation treatment to the exact area. The radiation itself was straightforward, and became routine. Carol would take her to the clinic early in the morning every weekday, and in fifteen minutes later her aunt would be finished. Aunt Sarah didn't suffer fatigue, and in fact the only side effect was the tanning of her breast, which she said was becoming quite leathery in appearance.

"I was talking to a nice woman, Judy, who's nearly finished her seven weeks of radiation," she said to Carol, "and she says her breast looks just like a football, sort of reddish-brown and a bit swollen."

"It doesn't stay that way, does it?"

"Heavens, no, dear. It's just like getting a really heavy dose of sun every day. Eventually, when the radiation stops, the skin gets back to normal."

Carol had organized her day so she could take her aunt in for treatment, drop her back at the house, and then go into work. This meant that Carol's morning run in the bush was moved to the evening, when she jogged on streets instead of trails, and her cherished time with a cup of coffee and the morning newspaper became a paper cup of pseudo-coffee dispensed by a machine at the clinic and a lightning scan of the paper while Aunt Sarah had her radiation treatment.

She followed with interest the way the media was dealing with the controlled information release that Superintendent Edgar, using the police PR department, was providing. The headlines had gone from, DEATHS POSSIBLY LINKED to MURDER-FOR-HIRE? POLICE BAFFLED.

When Carol had got in the morning of that particular headline, Edgar was incensed. *"Baffled*? We're not baffled. It doesn't reflect well on the Service. Carol, I want a retraction. You've got contacts. See to it."

"If we ask for a retraction, they'll just run with it harder."

Everything on his desk jumped as he slapped his hand down. "We've got to do something about the negative press we're getting. I want you to talk to that bloody reporter who broke the story in the first place, Vida Drake. I've cleared it with the Commissioner. Do a woman-to-woman with her, okay? Assure her, off the record, that an arrest is imminent.

Tell her we're taking time to build a watertight case. You know the drill."

Carol had run into Vida Drake several times before. She had a hard-won reputation as an investigative journalist of note, who would run a story to ground at any cost. In person she was a small middle-aged woman with a large mane of black hair filled with gray strands. Ignoring the dictates of fashion, for years she had worn flowing cotton dresses, often tie-dyed, and sandals.

She had laughed when Carol called to invite her into the Police Centre. "Ah, Carol, they've sicced you onto me, have they?"

"Vida, all I'm suggesting is a background chat, off the record..."

Vida had snorted, but agreed on the meeting. She arrived early, breezed into Carol's office, and plunked a miniature tape recorder on Carol's desk. "No recording," said Carol.

"Jesus, Carol, I don't take notes well, you know."

She snatched up the recorder and shoved it into her capacious bag. "I could be wired, you know."

"Are you?"

"No, but next time I will be."

Carol discussed Operation Pelican at length, without giving specific names. Vida listened, asked questions, and made acerbic comments about leaks in the Police Service. "The name Operation Pelican was out pretty well before you started to use it," she said.

"Someone in my team?"

Vida was amused. "Who would dare, Carol? I won't reveal my sources, but no one of yours." She leaned back in her chair. "So to sum up, you've got brother and sister psychos killing at will, is that what you're saying?"

"I presume they've suspended operations for the moment, with the heat we're putting on them."

"Alyce Mure, now Lyne, would be the female half of the

team, would she?" Vida gave Carol a smug smile. "Well, how am I doing?"

"Who's your informant?"

Vida wagged her finger. "No way, Carol, not unless I get something in return."

Carol looked at her reflectively. Vida's smile widened. "I didn't pick this up around the traps. Someone came to me with the information."

"Everything I've told you is only to be used as background," said Carol, "until we make an arrest. Then, if I possibly can, I'll let you know first."

"Deal," said Vida, getting ready to leave. "It's Dianne Beaton's ex-husband. Surprising how much animosity a simple divorce can cause, isn't it? He was pleased to tell me that while he and Dianne were married, he'd introduced her to Alyce." She handed Carol a business card. "No doubt you'd like to speak with him."

CHAPTER TWENTY

Dianne Beaton marched ahead of Carol and Bourke into a formal lounge room. There was no indication in the house that she was in financial trouble. The room was handsome, with everything in its place, including architectural magazines scattered with precision on a glass-topped table. Two crystal vases at either end of the mantelpiece held red roses. The colors in the room were warm, but the impression the room gave was as cold as the chill in the still, faintly scented air.

"Sit down," she said ungraciously. She waited until they had obeyed her preemptory command, then took a seat opposite them. "I suppose Sergeant Dent has been in touch with you."

"Sergeant Dent at the Manly station?"

She glowered at Carol. "There's more than one cop with that name?"

"He hasn't been in touch with us."

Dianne Beaton got up and paced around, the lines of her face, with its strong nose and angled jawline emphasized by the cold light flooding the room from floor-length windows. She paused at the fireplace, which was so pristine it seemed never to have been used for an open fire, although logs were set there ready to burn. Selecting a cigarette from an ebony box on the mantelpiece, she tapped it several times, then lit it with a matching ebony lighter. Carol noticed her hands were shaking.

"My stepmother, Evelyn, says she's going to contest the will." She sent Carol a challenging glance. "There are no grounds for her to do that. My father always promised he'd look after me." The tip of her cigarette flashed ruby red as she drew heavily on it. "I went over to Balgowlah to have it out with her."

A bitter smile touched her lips. "I underestimated Evelyn. She called the police and tried to have me arrested. Disturbing the peace, or trespass, or something like that. Not that it matters. After I told my side of the story, Sergeant Dent said he wasn't going to charge me with anything, but I assumed he'd report to you what had happened."

Dianne Beaton ground out her half-smoked cigarette, lit another, and sat down. "So why are you here, if it isn't because of that?"

"We've come from a meeting with your ex-husband."

"What?" Her pale face flushed. "Bruce? Why in the hell would you be seeing Bruce?"

"He had certain information," said Bourke blandly.

In the silence that followed, Carol could hear the muffled sound of a lawnmower, and the faint wail of a siren. At last Dianne Beaton said, "Information about what?"

"Alyce Lyne, nee Mure," said Carol.

Dianne Beaton drew on her cigarette, blew out a stream

184

of smoke, and said with what was clearly an effort at a conversational tone, "Bruce was into orchids. You know, those creepy looking flowers? So was Alyce. They both belonged to some stupid native orchid society based in the Blue Mountains. These fanatical people make me sick. It was orchids, orchids, orchids. No wonder my marriage broke up, I was playing second fiddle to a bloody plant."

Hiding a smile at this last comment, Carol asked, "When did you last speak with Alyce?"

"I don't remember. Ages ago. It's not as if we're friends. I don't think I've even got her current number." She tapped ash from her cigarette. "What's this all about? Why are you talking to Bruce, and what has Alyce got to do with anything?"

"Her husband died in a fall at Govetts Leap."

She shrugged. "I heard."

"There are some similarities with your father's case."

Again she shrugged. "They both fell off cliffs. So?"

Bourke took out his notebook and flipped over pages until he'd found his place. "In the weeks before your father's death you used several credit cards to make cash withdrawal in the amount of ten thousand dollars. Would you mind telling us what the money was for?"

Dianne Beaton jerked to her feet. "This is outrageous. How dare you pry into my affairs this way."

"Your father was murdered, Ms. Beaton," said Carol. "It's part of our investigation."

She took a deep breath. "The money was to pay off various debts. I've no intention of discussing it further. I'd like you leave."

At the door, she said, "You'd be very stupid to believe anything Bruce says. He hates me."

Walking to the car, Bourke said, "She's telling the truth about that, at least. Bruce Beaton certainly dislikes his ex-wife."

Carol nodded, remembering the venom with which Beaton had said, "Dianne would do anything to get her hands on her dad's money. When I heard that Alyce's husband had taken a dive, and then Trelawney did too, I knew it had to be more than a coincidence. And as soon as the word got around that you cops were interested in both cases, I knew I was right." With a sneer, he'd added, "Dianne would have pushed her dad herself if she'd had the guts."

Asked why he'd gone to a journalist with his suspicions, and not the police, Beaton had grunted derisively. "And you'd believe me? I've had enough trouble with you cops in the past. Every time Dianne and I had a fight — and it was often, I can tell you — she'd call the local station and say I'd hit her. And in almost every bloody instance you cops took her word against mine."

Bourke handed Carol several pages. "Here are the calls made from Dianne Beaton's house telephone and mobile phone for the past six months. No call to Alyce Lyne. And I had Anne check the orchid association. Alyce is still an active member. The secretary remembered that a woman called recently to ask for Alyce Lyne's telephone number, saying she was a friend who'd lost contact with Alyce after she'd left the Mountains. It could have been Dianne Beaton. If it was, she used a public phone to call Wollongong."

He handed her another, thicker bundle of pages. "Here are the telephone records for the last few months at Dexterous Unlimited. There's a single call to Alyce Lyne's number."

"It's not enough."

"It shows we're on the right track." Bourke grinned. "Terry's now convinced we should be staking out Penelope Neale twenty-four hours a day."

Carol groaned. "Zeal is all very well, but . . ."

"But how do you turn him off? Good question, Carol."

* * * * *

Later than evening, while Carol was catching up on the morning newspaper she'd barely scanned, Aunt Sarah, watching television, called out to her. "Come and look. Doesn't Dexterous Unlimited have something to do with one of your cases?"

Carol recognized the Dexterous reception area. Penelope Neale was being interviewed by an avuncular financial reporter, who was asking searching questions about the future of the company, now that two key partners had been killed. Penelope Neale was extremely drawn, and her voice shook as she tried to reassure the interviewer that the company was in sound financial shape and would be bringing out new products in the near future.

"She looks like she's falling to pieces," observed Aunt Sarah.

Penelope Neale had wanted to control the company, Carol thought, and now that she did, it appeared to be sinking beneath her.

The interview concluded with comments from the journalist that a probable offer of a take-over by a larger company was now in abeyance. As he finished, the camera focused on Penelope Neale's face. She seemed deeply shaken, and Carol wondered if Alyce and Ian were watching too. It wouldn't be reassuring for them to see one of their clients so close to a breakdown.

CHAPTER TWENTY-ONE

When the phone rang on Saturday night Aunt Sarah was reading a paperback mystery and Carol was grooming Sinker, who protested as a matter of course, but clearly was enjoying the attention. The sound of rain falling outside the window made everything seem warm and comfortable, and Carol frowned at the possibility that she was about to be called out on a homicide.

"Carol Ashton."

"I'm sorry to disturb you at home."

"It's all right, Anne, what is it?"

Anne Newsome sounded both apologetic and concerned. "I wouldn't have worried you, but I'm concerned about Terry."

"Terry Roham? What's he done?"

"We having a party, or rather, a barbecue. A group of us that is, and Terry swore that he'd be here, but he hasn't turned up."

Carol felt a throb of irritation. "Anne, you're calling me on Saturday night because Terry Roham is late for your party?"

Her sarcasm put a defensive note in Anne's voice. "I know it sounds silly, but . . ."

"But what?" Carol didn't hide her impatience.

"I don't want to get him into trouble . . ."

"Anne, this isn't like you. Just spit it out, for God's sake!"

Aunt Sarah looked up, surprised by Carol's vehemence.

Anne said in a rush, "Terry's been spending his spare time staking out Dexterous Unlimited, or rather, Penelope Neale. He knew you'd never agree to it, especially with the media problem at the moment. I told him it was a dumb thing to do, but he said he was sure that Ian Mure or his sister would turn up sooner or later. He's set himself up in his car with a camera loaded with ultra-sensitive film, a night scope, and a voice-activated recorder."

"Anne, you're not serious?"

"I know why he's doing it. Terry wants to impress you. He doesn't believe you think much of him, and he told me this was his chance to prove you wrong."

"Oh, great," said Carol, disgusted. "What do you expect me to do? Collect him and send him off to your party?"

There was silence at the other end of the line. Then Anne said, "I didn't know who else to call. Terry isn't answering his mobile phone."

"If he is on this misbegotten stake-out, he's probably forgotten that he's supposed to be there with you."

Carol was about to ring off, and was formulating a suitably irate comment to end the conversation, when Anne said, "Please believe me, Terry was really keen to be here tonight. And he hasn't forgotten, because we talked about it on the phone this afternoon. My sister, Rosie — he's really got a thing for her. There's no way he'd miss out on being here."

Anne paused, then said, "Do you want us to go look for him?"

"No way, Anne. The last thing I want is to have the media discover a bunch of you blundering around looking for someone on an unofficial stake-out. Leave it to me. When I find Terry, I'll tell him off for being such a total idiot, then I'll send him along to your barbecue."

Carol was irritated, but not concerned. Even so, a slight chill prickled her skin. It was obvious Anne was really worried, and it wasn't like her to be an alarmist.

She slammed down the phone. "I'm sorry, Aunt Sarah, I have to go out. I'll be back as soon as I can."

It was only sprinkling lightly when she got outside. She turned up the collar of her windjacket, cursing Roham for the inconvenience he was causing her. Thinking that Mark Bourke should know what Roham was up to, she called him as soon as she got into the car, but got the babysitter. Bourke and Pat were on their way to a restaurant, and the teenager promised she'd call him there with Carol's message. Carol made sure she wrote everything down, then rang off.

God, she was going to tear strips off Terry Roham when she found him. Single-handedly he could compromise the whole operation with his unauthorized stakeout. The media were already baying after the harassment angle Dianne Beaton had fed to them. The Commissioner was demanding all officers keep a low profile. Superintendent Edgar was fulminating at full bore. It would be a monumental fuck-up if Terry Roham was caught stalking a apparently innocent member of the public.

The rain petered out as she turned down the street that led to the industrial park where Dexterous Unlimited was situated. Snapping off the wipers, Carol mentally ran through exactly what she'd say to Roham when she found him. He was going to regret that he'd ever been born by the time she finished with him.

The area was deserted. Street lamps sat in pools of light separated by great areas of darkness. Carol was sure there would be security, but it probably consisted of a drive-by every few hours by a bored guy working for a private patrol company.

For the first time Carol realized how isolated this area was out of work hours, and how vulnerable Penelope Neale would be coming home after dark. Carol reached behind her to touch the reassuring contours of the sub-compact Glock she wore holstered in the small of her back. After an attack some time ago she'd got into the habit of carrying a concealed weapon whenever she left the house, even if it was to go jogging.

She'd intended to drive in and park near Terry's car, haul him out of it, tell him exactly what she thought of him, and send him on his way, but a sudden sense of caution prevailed. In this deserted blackness anything seemed possible. If was highly unlikely, but what if Terry wasn't barking up the wrong tree? What if Ian and Alyce did intend to silence Penelope Neale?

Carol drove past the entrance to the complex, turned out her lights and coasted to a stop a hundred meters down the road away from any illumination. She set her phone to vibrate, not give a betraying noise, and, after making sure the interior lights didn't come on when she opened the door, she got out into the damp, dark air. She pushed the door closed with a faint click, wedged the keys in the pocket of her jeans so they wouldn't rattle, shoved her phone in her back pocket, and, feeling faintly ridiculous, took out the Glock and held the little gun in her hand as she walked back toward the entrance, her sneakers making only a faint sound on the wet road.

The industrial park was lit, but not brightly, and the landscaping provided many bushes for cover. As she worked her way toward Dexterous, she was visualizing the complex as she'd seen it by day. It seemed to Carol that the most likely spot for Terry Rohan to position his car would be in the loading bay of the building adjoining Dexterous Unlimited, where he would be concealed, but could still see the outside iron stairs leading up to Penelope Neale's apartment.

Up to this point she had heard nothing but the soft sound of her own footsteps and the plop of heavy drops falling from sodden vegetation, but as she came to the entrance of the short alley running beside the Dexterous building, there was a sudden sound of pounding feet, a shout, and the hard revving of a car engine.

Carol stepped back into the cover of the head-high Oleanders that marked the entrance to the alley, squinting as headlights scintillated on the wet surface in front of her. Someone, silhouetted by the car roaring up behind, was running toward her.

The figure, legs pumping, had almost reached Carol when she recognized him. She saw a flash of Terry Roham's terrified face, eyes wide, mouth open. He veered, trying desperately to avoid the car behind him, but the vehicle was upon him. It didn't hit him square, but the force was enough fling him into the air like a life-size doll, arms and legs flying loose. He hit the ground with a sickening, meaty thump.

Brake lights flared, tires squealed as the car, an anonymous dark sedan, skidded past Terry's body. It halted, then did a three-point turn and came back to stop just short of its victim. In the headlights the unmoving, untidy bundle threw a long, grotesque shadow.

Ian Mure got out of the car without haste, and stood, hands on hips, looking down at the body. Carol, the Glock extended, took a step toward him.

Terry groaned.

"Not dead yet, mate?" Ian Mure gave a soft laugh as he pulled something from his pocket. "This'll do you."

Carol saw it clearly in the glare of the headlights — the weapon that had been used to hit Captain Trelawney before he was tossed to his death. It was a cosh, a deadly little blackjack that, with its springy shaft and weighted head, could crack a skull like an eggshell.

Ian Mure put the loop at the base of the cosh around his wrist, gripped it firmly and made a practice swing in the air. Then he went down on one knee, his shadow dancing crazily as he raised his arm to deliver the blow.

"I have a gun pointed at you," said Carol. "Please give me an excuse to pull the trigger." In the hip pocket of her jeans her phone vibrated.

He let his arm drop slowly, then got to his feet in one graceful movement. "Inspector Ashton," he said, peering into the semi-darkness where she stood. "Fancy meeting you here."

"Drop the cosh."

He didn't comply. "You're not going to shoot me," he said in a pleasant, conversational tone. "Not in cold blood."

The phone in her pocket stopped vibrating. It could have been Bourke calling back.

From a distance a voice called. "Ian? Where are you?"

He turned his head, looking back toward Dexterous. "Allie, this way. We have an unwelcome visitor, I'm afraid. Carol Ashton. She's got a gun on me."

To Carol he said, "Allie, too, is armed. Evens things up, you might say, but really, it's two against one. Not good odds for you, Inspector."

Terry groaned again, an awful, agonized sound. While they were standing here, Terry could be dying. Not taking her gaze from Ian Mure, Carol fished out her phone. She could see Alyce approaching, so she had to act fast. The phone was pre-programmed with the emergency services number, and Carol had to risk a glance to make sure she was pushing the correct keys.

That was all the opportunity Ian Mure required. He made a great, athletic leap, swinging the cosh above her head. Carol didn't step back, but braced herself and fired.

She was sure she'd hit him, but there was no effect. Carol darted away as his weapon came whistling down. "You bitch," he snarled.

A head shot would kill him, but she was determined to take Ian Mure alive. Then he was upon her. They fell, tangled together. Carol dropped the phone, rammed the Glock against Mure's leg and fired. He shrieked as his kneecap shattered.

An answering shriek came from his sister. "Don't hurt him, don't hurt Ian!"

Carol looked up to see a silver revolver trained unwaveringly upon her. "What have you done to him?" Alyce demanded, apparently oblivious that Carol still held the Glock.

"Oh, God," whispered Terry Roham. "Oh, God."

Carol saw the phone out of the corner of her eye. She groped around for it, not taking her focus from Alyce Lyne, seized it, and then got up slowly, phone in one hand, Glock in the other.

Amazingly, Ian Mure, by clinging to the front of the car, had managed to drag himself upright. He stood there on his good leg, blood pouring from his shattered knee, a red stain blossoming on his white shirt where Carol's first shot had hit home.

His face a pale mask of hatred and pain, he ground out, "Kill her slowly, Allie. Make her scream. Then shoot out those green eyes."

Alyce took his arm. "Ian, can you get yourself into the car? We have to get out of here. You need a doctor."

Mure was panting, and blood ran down his chin where he'd bitten his lip. "How's Penny?"

Alyce was matter-of-fact. "I gave her the K. She's dying as we speak."

Watching the silver revolver, which Alyce still had trained on her, Carol took a step forward. If each of them fired, both shots could be fatal. Carol wasn't gambler enough to take that chance, not if she had an alternative.

She and Alyce were two meters apart, too far to consider

disarming her. Carol said, "Alyce, your brother's chest is filling with blood. Soon he won't be able to breathe. He'll die if he doesn't get medical attention, fast. Let me call for an ambulance."

Ian Mure's mouth hung open as he dragged in great, whooping breaths. "Kill them both, and then let's get away."

Alyce put up her chin, steadied her aim on Carol's head. Carol said, "Your brother's dying. Don't you care?"

As if on cue, Ian Mure shuddered, then collapsed face down on the wet road.

"Ian!"

A split second was all Carol needed. She took a stride, and with the side of her hand delivered a sweeping blow to Alyce's wrist. The silver revolver spun out of her fingers and skidded away under the car.

Alyce didn't notice. She fell to her knees to cradle her brother's head. "Ian! Ian!"

As if in benediction, the rain began to fall.

CHAPTER TWENTY-TWO

Bourke drove into the industrial park almost simultaneously with three ambulances and two patrol cars. While Terry and Ian Mure were receiving urgent attention, and Alyce Lyne, pleading to stay with her brother, was handcuffed and put into the back of a patrol car, Carol and Bourke led the third ambulance team and a uniformed officer with a mini battering ram at a run to Penelope Neale's apartment.

She was slumped in a chair, deeply unconscious, her respiration laboring.

"I think it's ketamine, or something similar," said Carol.

Despite all attempts to stabilize her, it was clear Penelope Neale's condition was deteriorating fast. Before the stretcher had reached the bottom flight of the colored metal stairs, she had died.

Carol went with Bourke to the hospital where Terry Roham and Mure had been taken. Terry had concussion, a broken leg and cracked pelvis, plus sundry bruises and lacerations. The left side of his face, which had come in violent contact with the surface of the road, was scraped raw.

He was barely conscious when they went in to see him. "Did you get the camera?" he mumbled.

"We found it, Terry."

"Got shots of them both. Evidence . . ." He closed his eyes.

"Good work," Carol said, although she wasn't sure Terry could hear her.

"He'll live," his doctor announced. "Eventually be as good as new. The other one" — he made a face — "is touch and go."

To Carol Bourke said, "Forget touch, I hope it's go."

"We need Ian Mure, Mark. We've got at least five, probably more, people to prosecute, and he can provide all the evidence we need."

"Sweet Alyce can do that."

"Ian's the more conceited and arrogant of the two. He'll love boasting how clever he's been. He'll confess to everything in detail to demonstrate his superiority."

Within seven days Ian Mure was off the critical list, and improving by the hour. Alyce, remanded on murder charges, continued to send a stream of messages to her brother, although communication between the two was vetoed, so he wasn't permitted to see them.

Some weeks later, the multiple cases against Ian Mure and Alyce Lyne were taking shape. Prosecutions against eight others, including Dianne Beaton and Roger Bruehl, were well advanced, helped by the discovery of an encrypted file on Ian Mure's computer that detailed the intermediaries who had acted as contacts between the Mures and their clients. It had been, as Bourke had originally surmised, by word-of-mouth, with a subtle approach being made to a possible client once the person had clearly indicated the desire to be permanently rid of someone.

Carol had applied for five days leave, and was spending it in Canberra with Leota. First, she had to dispatch Aunt Sarah, who had received an all clear from her doctor, and was returning home to the Blue Mountains, coming back to Sydney only for final sittings with Yancey Blake, who was talking of submitting the painting for a national portrait competition.

"Cruel punishment," remarked Carol to Aunt Sarah as she helped her pack, "to separate Alyce from her brother. After herself, the only person in the world as important to Alyce is Ian Mure. And he feels the same way. It's likely, apart from the on-going legal proceedings, they'll never see each other again."

"They had so much," said Aunt Sarah. "Youth, and health, and intelligence. I'll never understand why they threw it all away."

As Carol, carrying her aunt's suitcase, was following Aunt Sarah to the front door, the phone rang. "Let the machine pick up," said Carol. "I'm officially gone from the office and if there's an emergency, I don't want to know about it."

The answering machine clicked on after four rings. Carol's voice advised that she couldn't come to the phone, and to leave a message.

"Sorry I missed you, Carol," said Ren Downing. "Gemma and I have been talking about this, and we've agreed it's a terrific idea. I don't know if we can persuade you to leave the Police Service, but I hope we can. We're offering you a partnership in the company. How does Downing, Pate and Ashton strike you? Sounds good to me. Call back when you get a chance, and we can discuss it."

She put the suitcase down as her aunt swung around to stare at her. "Carol? Would you?"

"Don't ask," said Carol. "I really don't know."

ABOUT THE AUTHOR

CLAIRE McNAB is the author of fourteen Detective Inspector Carol Ashton mysteries: *Lessons in Murder, Fatal Reunion, Death Down Under, Cop Out, Dead Certain, Body Guard, Double Bluff, Inner Circle, Chain Letter, Past Due, Set Up, Under Suspicion, Death Club,* and *Accidental Murder.* She has written two romances, *Under the Southern Cross* and *Silent Heart,* and has co-authored a self-help book, *The Loving Lesbian,* with Sharon Gedan. She is the author of three Denise Cleever thrillers, *Murder Undercover, Death Understood,* and *Out of Sight.* The fourth Denise Cleever thriller, *Recognition Factor,* will be published in fall of 2002.

In her native Australia Claire is known for her crime fiction, plays, children's novels, and self-help books.

Now permanently residing in Los Angeles, she teaches fiction writing in the UCLA Extension Writers' Program. She makes it a point to return to Australia once a year to refresh her Aussie accent.

Publications from
BELLA BOOKS, INC.
The best in contemporary lesbian fiction

P.O. Box 201007   Ferndale, MI 48220
Phone: 800-729-4992
www.bellabooks.com

ACCIDENTAL MURDER: 14th Detective Inspector Carol
Ashton Mystery by Claire McNab. 208 pp.Carol Ashton
tracks an elusive killer.   ISBN 1-931513-16-3 $12.95

SEEDS OF FIRE:Tunnel of Light Trilogy, Book II by Karin
Kallmaker writing as Laura Adams. 274 pp. Intriguing
sequel to *Slight of Hand.*   ISBN 1-931513-19-8 $12.95

DRIFTING AT THE BOTTOM OF THE WORLD by
Auden Bailey. 280 pp. Beautifully written first novel set
in Antarctica.   ISBN 1-931513-17-1 $12.95

STREET RULES: A DETECTIVE FRANCO MYSTERY
by Baxter Clare. 304 pp. Gritty, fast-paced mystery with
compelling Detective L.A. Franco   ISBN 1-931513-14-7 $12.95

CLOUDS OF WAR by Diana Rivers. 288 pp. Women
unite to defend Zelindar!   ISBN 1-931513-12-0 $12.95

OUTSIDE THE FLOCK by Jackie Calhoun. 220 pp.
Searching for love, Jo finds temptation. ISBN 1-931513-13-9 $12.95

WHEN GOOD GIRLS GO BAD: A Motor City Thriller by
Therese Szymanski. 230 pp. Brett, Andi, and Allie join
forces to stop a serial killer.   ISBN 1-931513-11-2 $12.95

DEATHS OF JOCASTA: The Second Micky Night Mystery
by J.M. Redmann. 408 pp. Sexy and intriguing Lambda
Literary Award nominated mystery   ISBN 1-931513-10-4 $12.95

LOVE IN THE BALANCE by Marianne K. Martin. 256 pp.
The classic lesbian love story, back in print!
                                       ISBN 1-931513-08-2 $12.95

THE COMFORT OF STRANGERS by Peggy J. Herring.
272 pp. Lela's work was her passion . . . until now.
                                       ISBN 1-931513-09-0 $12.95

CHICKEN by Paula Martinac. 208 pp. Lynn finds that the
only thing harder than being in a lesbian relationship is
ending one.   ISBN 1-931513-07-4 $11.95

TAMARACK CREEK by Jackie Calhoun. 208 pp. An intriguing story of love and danger.   ISBN 1-931513-06-6 $11.95

DEATH BY THE RIVERSIDE: The First Micky Knight Mystery by J.M. Redmann. 320 pp. Finally back in print, the book that launched the Lambda Literary Award winning Micky Knight mystery series.   ISBN 1-931513-05-8 $11.95

EIGHTH DAY: A Cassidy James Mystery by Kate Calloway. 272 pp. In the eighth installment of the Cassidy James mystery series, Cassidy goes undercover at a camp for troubled teens.   ISBN 1-931513-04-X $11.95

MIRRORS by Marianne K. Martin. 208 pp. Jean Carson and Shayna Bradley fight for a future together.
ISBN 1-931513-02-3 $11.95

THE ULTIMATE EXIT STRATEGY: A Virginia Kelly Mystery by Nikki Baker. 240 pp. The long-awaited return of the wickedly observant Virginia Kelly.   ISBN 1-931513-03-1 $11.95

FOREVER AND THE NIGHT by Laura DeHart Young. 224 pp. Desire and passion ignite the frozen Arctic in this exciting sequel to the classic romantic adventure *Love on the Line*.   ISBN 0-931513-00-7 $11.95

WINGED ISIS by Jean Stewart. 240 pp. The long-awaited sequel to *Warriors of Isis* and the fourth in the exciting Isis series.   ISBN 1-931513-01-5 $11.95

ROOM FOR LOVE by Frankie J. Jones. 192 pp. Jo and Beth must overcome the past in order to have a future together.   ISBN 0-9677753-9-6 $11.95

THE QUESTION OF SABOTAGE by Bonnie J. Morris. 144 pp. A charming, sexy tale of romance, intrigue, and coming of age.   ISBN 0-9677753-8-8 $11.95

SLEIGHT OF HAND by Karin Kallmaker writing as Laura Adams. 256 pp. A journey of passion, heartbreak and triumph that reunites two women for a final chance at their destiny.   ISBN 0-9677753-7-X $11.95

MOVING TARGETS: A Helen Black Mystery by Pat Welch. 240 pp. Helen must decide if getting to the bottom of a mystery is worth hitting bottom.   ISBN 0-9677753-6-1 $11.95

CALM BEFORE THE STORM by Peggy J. Herring. 208 pp. Colonel Robicheaux retires from the military and comes out of the closet.   ISBN 0-9677753-1-0 $12.95

OFF SEASON by Jackie Calhoun. 208 pp. Pam threatens Jenny and Rita's fledgling relationship. ISBN 0-9677753-0-2 $11.95

WHEN EVIL CHANGES FACE: A Motor City Thriller by Therese Szymanski. 240 pp. Brett Higgins is back in another heart-pounding thriller.   ISBN 0-9677753-3-7 $11.95

Visit
Bella Books
at

www.bellabooks.com